THE LADY'S DISGRACE

A MARRIAGE MART MAYHEM NOVEL

THE LADY'S DISGRACE

A MARRIAGE MART MAYHEM NOVEL

CALLIE HUTTON

Entangled Publishing, LLC
2614 South Timberline Road
Suite 109
Fort Collins, CO 80525
Visit our website at www.entangledpublishing.com.

Scandalous is an imprint of Entangled Publishing, LLC.

Edited by Erin Molta
Cover design by Liz Pelletier

ISBN 978-1502497819

Manufactured in the United States of America

First Edition September 2014

To newlyweds Scott & Jessica, who when I wrote this were awaiting the birth of their twin boys.

Chapter One

May, 1815
London

Lady Abigail Lacey sighed and rolled over on her bed, staring at the canopy above her. She was tired of feeling bereft. Tired of feeling sorry for herself, tired of hating her erstwhile betrothed, Darius, Earl of Redgrave, and the woman he eloped with two weeks ago. But most of all she was tired of her self-imposed prison. How had her sister Marion endured it for two years while she'd been grieving her husband?

She was much too energetic a person to spend her days in ennui. In the past two weeks, she'd gone through all the stages of hurt, rage, and depression. The heartbreak would be with her for a long time to come, but now she just wanted to get on with her life. Except there was no life to get on with. Her sisters had stopped in to visit with her, keeping her current on the mockery her reputation had become.

Not that they did it to torture her, they loved her too much. But Abigail had insisted they tell her everything the *ton* was saying about her *disgrace*. She huffed. *Her* disgrace? She'd done nothing wrong, except pick a worthless bounder to become betrothed to.

Apparently the *ton* was rampant with jealousy over the Lacey girls. That one of them fell so low as to have a fiancé hie off with another woman, practically leaving her at the altar, was just too much. Ladies who had viewed the wealth, beauty, and success of the family with envy, now found it amusing to poke fun at one of them. It would be quite some time before this *on dit* was laid to rest.

Thinking of the cad at the center of this mess replaced her apathy with pain once again. She swiped at the lone tear that rolled down her cheek. Never would she have believed the man she had loved, indeed had waited for her whole life, would betray her in this fashion.

Well, one thing was certain. If she was able to get anyone worthwhile to offer for her in the future, she would grab the chance and never expect—or even want—love. No more waiting for the right man to come along and sweep her off her feet. She'd been swept off her feet, and dropped ignominiously on her arse.

Thank you, no.

Perhaps some shopkeeper or chimney sweep would be willing to take her off her brother's hands—if he paid him enough. She rolled to her stomach and propped her head up with her hands, sighing once more at her returning self-pity. In any event, should anyone have her, she'd insist on a platonic marriage.

No, that wouldn't work. If she couldn't have love in her marriage, she would at least want a home of her own, and children. Unfortunately, offspring only came about if one allowed one's husband to visit one's bed. She'd have to think that one over more carefully. Except, with the shredded reputation she had right now, she doubted any worthwhile offers would be forthcoming, anyway. Back to the shopkeepers and chimney sweeps. Perhaps a Bow Street Runner or tavern keeper.

Restless, she rolled onto her back again. There was always next year. By then her scandal would have been replaced by something more exciting. Hopefully, that is. The *ton* had a long memory.

. . .

The Duke of Manchester slammed his palm down on the desk, causing his wife and mother to jump. "I will not have it! I refuse to allow another sister to lock herself away in her room. We put up with that nonsense for two years with Marion, and I will not permit the same situation with Abigail."

"Drake dear, calm yourself. Please." His wife, Penelope, rubbed gently on the infant's back she held snug against her chest. "You'll upset the baby."

Drake blew out a huge breath of air and collapsed into his seat, running his fingers through his hair. "Sorry, my love. But it's been two weeks."

"Two weeks of pain and humiliation for your sister," the Dowager Duchess of Manchester remarked.

"Damn that Redgrave. He had better not return to

London from Gretna Green with his new *wife,* or I shall be forced to beat him to a pulp for what he did to Abigail.

"What are we to do? Her reputation is in tatters. She'll never receive another suitable offer." He turned, his jaw tightening. "She has become the laughingstock of the *ton.*"

"I'm sure it is not all that bad." His mother's pursed lips and strained countenance belied her words.

"Yes, Mother. It *is* that bad. Abigail has not had one decent caller since Redgrave absconded. If one more fortune hunter shows up on my doorstep I will personally grab him by the scruff of the neck and hurl him down the steps." He shoved his chair back and began to pace, his insides in a knot at this latest problem with yet another sister under his guidance.

The relief at having at least one of them headed to the altar had been fleeting. Engaged one minute, abandoned the next.

"Apparently, the word being spread in the highest circles is that the only thing Abigail has to offer a man is her dowry. Damnation, the girl did nothing wrong! And now, Sybil and Sarah tell me they are beginning to notice a distinct drop in the amount of callers they have. Mary, too."

"Well, there is only one thing to be done. And we all know what that is," his mother said. "We must get Abigail married and out of London."

"Madam, were you not fully engaged the last three seasons when *your daughter* turned down one offer after another? Do you not remember the numerous discussions over the dinner table where she waxed poetically about holding out for a love match? And where in heaven's name am I to find this paragon—a man who doesn't care about her predicament, isn't only interested in her money, and will make her, if not happy, at least content?"

Drake sat slumped in his chair, and Penelope kissed him on top of his head. "Dear, you are getting yourself into a stew. It will all work out. You and I have a love match. Why shouldn't your sisters hold out for the same thing?

"I am taking Robert upstairs. Then I will arrange for tea. Perhaps we can discuss this then, in a calmer manner."

Drake's gaze followed the gentle sway of his wife's hips as she left the room, his lips twitching as she banged her knee on a table by the door.

"I do not understand why everyone keeps moving furniture about," she mumbled as she hurried through the doorway, clutching her precious bundle tightly. He and his mother grinned at each other. Penelope's clumsiness was legendary in the family.

"Is it so appalling that Abigail wanted for herself what you and Penelope have?" his mother asked softly.

"She just picked the wrong man. And when I get my hands on that . . ." Unable to express himself in words suitable for his mother's ears, he clamped his mouth shut.

"It would do us well to begin a list of possible husbands for Abigail."

"And what makes you think she will go along with this plan, given her attitude the past few years?"

"The situation has changed. Abigail is a smart woman. She knows her appeal has dropped significantly due to her circumstances."

"Circumstances she had no control over."

"Dwelling on that will do us—and her—no good. We must deal with the problem at hand."

The Manchester House butler, Stevens, quietly entered the room, a small card in his hand. "Your Grace, a caller has arrived."

Drake's eyebrows rose as he read the card. "Of course, send him in." He glanced up at his mother. "Joseph Fox. I haven't seen him since before my wedding."

"Didn't you travel with him to Manchester Manor when Marion made her first trip from her room last year?"

Drake nodded. He had been accompanying his sister and his now-wife to the Manor when they had run into the rector at an Inn where they'd stopped for luncheon.

Marion had spent two years in her room mourning her husband. As a house guest for the Season, Penelope had befriended his sister, and with her encouragement Marion had taken steps to resume a normal life.

He frowned when he recalled how taken Joseph had been with Penelope during that visit to the Manor, and had, in fact, asked Drake's permission to request her hand in marriage.

The memory of how angry he had been at Joseph's request still made his muscles tighten. He should have realized then that he was already in love with Penelope. Although when Joseph had suggested such a thing to him, Drake had erupted in anger. Panic, most likely, since at the time he had had no use for love.

"Manchester. Good to see you." Joseph entered the room in a swirl of energy and friendliness. He extended his hand. "I see married life agrees with you."

"Indeed it does."

Joseph turned and bowed before the dowager duchess, taking her raised hand. "A delight to see you again, Your

Grace. You are looking well, as always."

"Thank you, Joseph. You appear to be doing quite well yourself."

Drake sat as he waved Joseph to a chair. "To what do we owe the pleasure of your visit?"

"I had some business in Town, and since I had a bit of free time, I thought to stop in and see how you are all faring."

They turned as the door opened, and a footman carried in a tray laden with tea and small sandwiches.

"Will you stay for tea?" the dowager asked.

"Absolutely. I would love a cup, and how is your lovely wife?" Joseph asked Drake as he took a cup from the dowager's hand. "I understand from my parents that you are the proud parents of a son?"

"Yes, indeed. Robert Cyril Lacey, Marquess of Stafford, made his presence known the third day of March this year. He and my wife are doing well." He paused and glanced toward the doorway. "Ah, here is my duchess now."

"Joseph!" In Penelope's enthusiasm to hug the rector, she tripped on the claw foot of the dowager's chair and crashed into Joseph's chest.

"Oh, dear. Please excuse me." She righted herself, smoothing her skirts and adjusting her spectacles, her face a bright red.

Accustomed to her lack of coordination, Joseph merely smiled and took hold of her hands. "You are looking quite lovely, Your Grace. And congratulations on the birth of the new heir."

She patted her hair and took a seat next to her mother-in-law on the sofa. "Thank you. Unfortunately, you missed him. I have just now returned from settling him in the nursery."

"Ah, yes. The family that deals with their own children. Most refreshing among the Quality." Mirth danced in his eyes.

"What brings you to London?" Penelope asked.

Joseph placed his cup on the low table in front of him and leaned back in his chair, crossing a booted foot over his knee. "I have decided it is time our village children had a proper school. I realize most of the youngsters are needed at home to help, but I am hoping to establish a routine so they are able to come for at least a few hours each day."

"That's a wonderful idea, Joseph!" Penelope accepted the serviette Drake held out to her and wiped her bodice where her tea had dripped.

"Thank you. The only drawback, of course, is money to build a school. For now, I can certainly teach several of them in my home. However, a separate building that they know belongs to them would encourage parents' acceptance of the project, and allow us to draw in more children."

"I will be more than happy to make a donation."

"Thank you so much." Joseph nodded in Drake's direction.

"I will have my man of business take care of it."

"I have come to realize as I delve more into the project that a steady source of income will be needed to pay teachers–eventually–and supply books and necessary items for the students. I don't want the parents to be burdened with the cost. I'm afraid if the choice between school fees and food for the table arose, like any sensible parent, food would come first.

"Although my maternal grandmother's property

provides a modest income to me, it will not be enough to keep the school afloat in the long run, without patrons."

• • •

Joseph studied Penelope and Drake, and the glances they cast at each other, their love apparent to an observer. Some day he hoped to have a wife of his own. One who looked upon him as Penelope did her husband.

"How are all your sisters? Marion? Is she dealing better with her loss?"

"Marion has returned to a normal social life. Mary, Sybil and Sarah are still chasing away suitors." Drake gave a half smile.

"And Abigail?"

The silence in the room was deafening. The two women glanced furtively at each other, then became enthralled with their teacups. Drake cleared his throat and seemed to search for words.

Alarmed, Joseph asked, "Is Abigail ill?"

"No. Not ill."

"Then what it is, man? Has she been injured?" He grew more concerned as no one in the room seemed able to form answers to his questions. He'd always considered Abigail the brightest star of the Lacey girls. Although he'd found her an annoying child when they were all growing up back in Donridge Heath, he had spoken with her several times in the last few years whenever the family had returned to the country. She was a lovely woman, always pleasant, with a sunny disposition. Had it not been for the difference in their station, he would have asked permission to court her.

"Abigail has had a bit of a problem."

Lips tightened, Joseph eased to the edge of his chair and nodded at Drake to continue.

"She became engaged to the Earl of Redgrave in March."

Joseph brushed aside the niggling of disappointment. "That is good news." When no one acknowledged his remark, he added, "Isn't it?"

"Not quite. It seems two weeks ago Redgrave eloped to Gretna Green with Lady Priscilla, Lord Rumbold's daughter."

"Say he wouldn't do something so despicable!"

"Afraid so. He apparently had been," Drake stopped and glanced at his mother and wife, "involved in a relationship with the girl before he became betrothed to my sister, and Lady Priscilla turned up in a family way."

All the blood left his face, leaving Joseph a bit lightheaded at this news. As much as he didn't like to think of Abigail betrothed to another, this was a terrible thing to happen to the girl. She must be devastated. "How is Abigail handling this?"

"Not well, I'm afraid. When she received the note from Redgrave, she retired to her room and has remained there since. Reclusion seems to be a favorite method of my sisters in managing pain."

Joseph shook his head in disbelief. To so dishonor a lady—two ladies in fact—was abhorrent.

"I intended to call him out when he returned, but my intelligent wife reminded me of my duty to family which would be in jeopardy if I were dead or forced to flee the country. But that doesn't mean I can't find some way to pay him back for his perfidy."

"I don't know what to say. I feel absolutely horrible for Abigail. And I'm sure this has been the subject of much gossip."

"Indeed. To put it bluntly, my sister's prospects have dimmed. The only men who are now paying her mind are fortune hunters who believe they would do us a favor by taking her off our hands." He smiled wryly. "By putting *their hands* on her money."

"Perhaps you should send Abigail off to the country."

"That would solve the immediate problem, but I need a long-term solution. I'm sure by next Season the gossip will have died down, but she would be one more year closer to being on the shelf."

Joseph's gut tightened at the thought of anyone considering Abigail *on the shelf* regardless of how many Seasons she saw. "Such a barbarous system we subject our young ladies to. Yet gentlemen are permitted years to avoid matrimony, with no consequences."

"Good heavens, you sound like my sisters."

"Your sisters are very intelligent young women, Manchester. But you're right, of course. Abigail is in a bit of a dilemma. If there's anything I can do to help, please let me know. Abigail has always been one of my favorite people."

Manchester somberly studied his desktop for a few minutes, the only sounds in the room the clicking of china. Suddenly the man straightened in his chair and stared straight at Joseph with such a piercing look that he shifted in his seat.

"Mother," Drake never glanced in her direction, "would you and Penelope mind leaving us for a few minutes?"

The dowager hesitated slightly, her eyes darting between the two men. "Of course, we wouldn't mind." She turned to Penelope, the women regarding each other with raised eyebrows.

They rose in unison, and adjusting their skirts, took their leave, their arms joined and heads together in a whispered discussion as they strolled to the door.

Once the door latch sounded, Drake left his seat, and clasping his hands behind his back, paced in a circle around his desk, causing Joseph to twist and turn to continue watching him.

"Manchester, you're making me dizzy."

Drake looked up in surprise. Almost as if he'd forgotten Joseph's presence.

"Sorry. Woolgathering. Trying to settle things in my mind."

"I assume there is a reason you asked your mother and wife to leave the room? Did you wish to say something about Redgrave that is unfit for ladies' ears?" Trying to lighten the suddenly grim atmosphere, Joseph's smile faded as Drake continued to study him as if he were a bug under a microscope.

"Tell me a little bit about your church."

Of all the things he might have expected to hear from his old friend, this question was certainly not one of them. His church? What the devil was he about?

After studying Drake for a few moments, realizing the man was serious in his question, Joseph answered. "St. Gertrude is a thriving parish. It's in Addysby End, which you know is the village south of Manchester Manor. Most of my parishioners are farmers and shopkeepers." He stopped and narrowed his eyes. "What are you about? Why in the middle of discussing your family's problems do you want to know about my church?"

Drake waved his hand. "Just bear with me for a little bit." He returned to his seat, clasping his hand together, tapping his lips with his index fingers. "What about this school? How close are you to raising the necessary funds?"

"My benefactors are few. But I've just started to visit with potential patrons. If necessary, I could dip into my investments, although the bulk of the money is tied up until I marry, or reach my thirty-fifth year."

Had these questions come from anyone but the Duke of Manchester, Joseph would have been sure the man had taken leave of his senses. But Drake was much too sharp to make inane conversation so shortly after revealing his family's predicament.

"And I believe you mentioned needing a steady source of income to sustain the school?"

"Yes. Although I am sure my parishioners will contribute items that can be bartered for school supplies. They have too much pride to take something for free. In any event, I am confident it will all work out."

When Drake continued to stare at the papers stacked on his desk, Joseph ventured, "May I ask why the sudden interest in my church and school?"

"In due time." Drake leaned back. "Am I correct in assuming you have not married since I saw you last?"

Joseph frowned and shook his head.

"Betrothed?"

"Noooo." He dragged the word out, more confused than ever. Questions about his church, the school, now his marital status? If he'd been baffled before, now he was totally flummoxed. Unless Manchester was headed in a direction Joseph would never have guessed. Or hoped for. His heartbeat sped up.

"As you are aware, my family has always held you–and your parents–in high regard."

Although his church was in the village about thirty miles south of Manchester Manor, Joseph's father, the elder Mr. Fox, was rector to the Manchester family's church in Donridge Heath.

Joseph hesitated. "I am pleased to hear that. And both I and my parents have always hoped you and your family regard us as friends. Despite our differences in rank."

"Good, good. Glad to hear that."

"What is going on here, Manchester?"

He looked up abruptly, obviously surprised to have his thoughts interrupted. "What do you mean?"

"I mean, you asked your wife and mother to leave the room. You've peppered me with questions about my church and the school I hope to build. Then you talk about the relationship between our families. I am wondering what it is that you're trying very hard not to say."

"Yes, you're right. I should just get on with it."

Drake fidgeted with his pen, taking it out of the holder, slipping it back in again. The man was obviously nervous. Definitely not usual circumstances for Drake. Dare he hope his childhood friend was about to suggest Joseph's well-hidden desire?

"What do you think of Abigail?"

"I think she's a wonderful woman, and I am distressed at her predicament."

"Good. Because there's something I want to ask you."

Finally. His stomach in knots, he motioned with his hand for Manchester to proceed. Trying very hard not to anticipate Drake's words, he held his breath.

Manchester leaned forward, his elbows on his desk. "Please give serious consideration to my suggestion."

"I'm listening."

"I would like you to marry my sister."

Joseph sat back, all the breath leaving his body. Exhilaration mixed with shock. Despite what he'd hoped Drake would say, he still would not have been any more surprised if the man had jumped up, taken off all his clothes, and dashed around the room spouting poetry.

Marry Abigail? The one woman he never thought would be his?

Chapter Two

A tap on Abigial's bedchamber door drew her from her musings. "Yes?"

The door opened, and Drake stuck his head in. "May I visit with you?"

Abigail shifted from the mattress and stood, adjusting her skirts. "Certainly."

"How are you feeling today?"

Abigail smiled. "You mean am I still soaking my pillow with tears?"

He grimaced at her astute perception.

"No more crying, Drake. I'm finished with feeling sorry for myself."

"That is good news. I worried that you would end up locked in your room like Marion."

"I'm not Marion. If I spend much more time cosseted here, I would be a candidate for Bedlam."

He cleared his throat, and waved her toward the daybed

in the corner of the room. "Can we sit for a moment?"

Once they settled, he turned to her and took her hands. "I have an idea."

"My, you look so serious. Am I to be relegated to a nunnery?" Her heart skipped a beat when he didn't laugh. Surely he wouldn't suggest an abbey? Good heavens, had things really gotten that bad beyond this room?

"No. No nunnery. I—Well, mother and I—that is, and Penelope too—"

"Are you going to go down the line and mention everyone? I can save you time. This sounds like something the family has decided on."

"It is good to see your humor and spirit have returned."

She smiled wryly. "Go on, dear brother. You are stalling."

"Yes. Well. I have an idea to get you out of London, and settled where you will be, if not happy, at least content."

"The nunnery comes to mind once again."

"I have found you a husband," he blurted.

She stared at him aghast. "I hadn't realized I'd misplaced one."

"Be serious, Abigail."

"I am serious. Extremely so. I know I seem to be missing a betrothed, but surely you haven't been scouring the streets of London looking for a replacement?"

"You remember Addysby End's rector, Joseph Fox?"

"Of course I remember him. We all grew up together. His father is our rector. I've seen him many times over the years. What has he got to do with—" She stopped abruptly. "Oh, no. No, no, no, no, no. You can't mean your *found* husband is Joseph?"

"That is precisely what I mean." He drew himself up.

"What is wrong with the man?"

Too stunned to form words, Abigail just stared at him. Joseph Fox had been her nemesis for years. As a child, she had had such a fancy for him that she had followed him and Drake around until they had become so annoyed with her that they'd tied her to a tree and sent Sybil to tell her mother where she was.

Despite the differences in their rank, Joseph had continued to hang about Manchester Manor every time both he and Drake were home from University. Joseph had grown into a handsome, virile man—with a bit of a devilish twinkle in his eyes, despite his higher calling.

The few times Abigail had tried to gain his attention as she'd approached her come-out, he had treated her as a little sister. Although the rejection had stung, once caught up in the whirl of her first Season, with all the balls, gowns, parties, and musicales, she'd forgotten all about her infatuation. Except for the few times they met in the village when he was there to visit his parents. He'd treated her with respect, but his eyes always seemed shuttered, as if attempting to hide something from her.

Now the man had agreed to marry her. Or had he?

She narrowed her eyes at her brother. "Have you spoken to Joseph about this?"

"Yes. He's downstairs right now."

"Here? Downstairs? Right now?"

"Very good, Abigail. It seems your ability to repeat words and phrases is top notch."

She viewed him with disgust. "Say you didn't summon him all the way from Addysby End to present this ridiculous proposition to him?"

"No, he is visiting London and was nice enough to call."

"He was 'nice enough to call?' You mean he just happened to stop in, you invited him for tea, and served up your sister?"

"That is enough, Abigail."

She slumped, closing her eyes. "I'm sorry."

"If you will calm yourself, I will explain how it all came about."

She shrugged.

"Redgrave has put you in an impossible situation."

She gave an unladylike snort.

"Through absolutely no fault of your own, your reputation has been tarnished. The way I see it, you can weather the storm, and eventually take your proper place in society. Which, given the *ton's* love of gossip, could take a while. Or you can marry someone you like and respect, and have a comfortable life. Love has been known to grow from more tenuous circumstances."

"I have no interest, whatsoever, in love. I've had my fill of it."

"Then this is not so terrible a suggestion?"

"No. I do want my own home and children. But why Joseph?"

"Why not? Do you have something against the man?"

Not wishing to dredge up old feelings of rejection, she shook her head.

"Then why not consider marrying him?"

Marriage to Joseph? Indeed, she did like and respect him. But the intimacy of marriage could very easily turn those feelings into something she no longer wanted. The hurt that love had the ability to inflict upon someone was not worth the few heady moments of elation. If she went along with this crazy scheme of her brother's, she would have to be extremely careful with her heart.

"What sort of inducement did you dangle in front of Joseph to take me off your hands?" Surely the man who thought of her as no more than a pesky little sister would not freely enter into a lifelong commitment without some type of boon.

"It was not an inducement as much as a way to solve both of your problems."

"I'm waiting."

"Joseph wants to open a school for the village children. He is in London to raise money for that very reason. Your dowry would more than cover the cost of the school, as well as provide an income to support the endeavor."

"Joseph is opening a school?" Suddenly the idea became more palatable. For some time now, the constant round of parties and balls had become tiresome. Her life seemed to lack purpose. She wanted to do something else with her energy, besides shopping for new gowns and fripperies. To be involved in something so worthwhile... "I will consider it. But I want to speak with Joseph first."

"Of course. He is waiting for you in the library. I told him either you or I would join him, depending on how amenable you were to this plan."

"Fine. Please tell him I will attend him shortly."

Drake nodded and left the room.

Abigail took a deep breath, and placed her hands on her chest where her breath caught. For the first time in two weeks she felt alive again. She could marry Joseph and have her own home. Nothing as grand as Manchester Manor, but somehow that no longer seemed important.

Her life would be one of fulfillment, of helping children have a better life. As a rector's wife, she would be in a position to use her boundless energy to good purpose. And one day there would be children of her own. Her thoughts came to a screeching halt as her stomach did a little flip. The begetting of those children was certainly something she would discuss with Joseph.

Yes. As long as she laid down rules to keep Joseph from believing there would ever be more to this arrangement than just two people working together, Drake's intriguing suggestion just might solve her dilemma.

She quickly washed her face and hands and smoothed back her hair, tying it at the nape with a ribbon. Time to face her future.

• • •

Joseph was sure the carpet beneath his feet in Manchester's study would be threadbare before Abigail arrived. He hadn't stopped pacing since Drake had informed him Abigail was amenable to the plan and would speak with him shortly.

It appeared in just moments, he would propose marriage to a woman who was far above him in rank and expect her to accept him. He'd firmly put her out of his mind when, as a blushing miss, she seemed to have developed a *tendre* for him. There hadn't been any reason to encourage her, since, as a duke's daughter, her family would see that she married well. And that did not mean to a rector of a modest church in an obscure village.

A light tap on the door caught his attention. Abigail

entered, hesitant at first. He gave her a warm smile, trying to put her at ease, even though his own heart was pounding in his chest.

She was just as lovely as he remembered. Shining, light brown hair with golden strands throughout. Her large whiskey-colored eyes looked on the world with a combination of curiosity and merriment, as if she held a great secret she was bursting to reveal. The little girl had turned into a curvy, sensuous woman. His mouth dried as she glided across the room, extending her arm.

"Joseph, it is good to see you."

Taking her hand, he touched his lips to the silky skin, then dropped it as if he'd been burned. "And you, as well, Lady Abigail."

She cocked her head to one side. "I guess given what we are here to discuss, we should discard the formality. Don't you agree?"

He nodded, and waved to the settee as if he were the host. "Won't you sit?"

Abigail cast him a sidelong glance, then smiled and settled on the sofa, smoothing her skirts. "My brother tells me you intend to start a school for the village children."

"Yes. It has been my desire for some time now. I think it is important for even the lower classes to be able to read, write, and do sums. It will open up new opportunities for them as adults."

"And my dowry will see that you are able to do that."

Once again, she'd put him off balance. Barely recovered from the jolt he'd received when he held her hand, she'd now plunged him into a swirl of emotions. Was she angry that her dowry would go to his cause? Did she see him only as another fortune hunter, eager to grasp her money, taking her to wife for that purpose only?

"There is no point in denial, is there?" he said.

"No matter. From what Drake has told me, we both get something from this arrangement."

Joseph took her hand in his. "I would hope this *arrangement* will bring some happiness to the both of us. I know of your recent disappointment, and am very sorry for it."

"Yes. Well. If we are to move forward with this, there are a few things we need to discuss." She pulled her hand away and began to pace in front of him.

He was surprised at her abrupt change of subject. Although he imagined it would pain her to speak of her betrothed's deception. Drake had mentioned that Abigail had been holding out for love. No doubt she was broken hearted and didn't wish to dwell on what she had lost.

"I must tell you first up that I will always think of you as a friend. Frankly, I do not want more than that from this. . .marriage."

Not too happy with the direction in which she seemed to be going, he merely stared at her.

"I also would like to make it clear straight off that I have no interest in the marriage bed."

"What?"

She drew herself up, and stopped the infernal pacing. "This is to be a marriage of convenience."

Joseph reached for her hand and pulled her down next to him. "No."

"What do you mean, no?"

"It is not a difficult word. Two letters, one meaning. No."

"I insist that—"

Not knowing what else to do to shut her up, he leaned forward and kissed her. Her plump lips were warm and moist, and tasted sweet. Her surprise kept her stiff, and then for the briefest moment, she relaxed and kissed him back. Then she placed her hands on his chest and shoved.

"Stop."

"No marriage of convenience."

She sat back and smoothed her hair. "You didn't let me finish." She shifted away from him, allowing plenty of space. Was she afraid her words would provoke another kiss? He braced himself for what would come next.

"I want children."

Joseph leaned back and crossed his arms, trying very hard to hide his mirth. "Abigail, I know you are an innocent miss, but there is no way I believe you are unaware of how children come about."

"Of course not." Her lovely complexion turned an interesting shade of red.

"Then how can you say in one breath you want a marriage of convenience, and in the next, speak of children?"

"What I intended to say was I will permit your *attentions* until I am with child. Then I would hope as a gentleman, you will honor my wishes to not continue with ... you know." She waved her hand between the two of them.

He'd never heard anything so absurd in his entire life. Have sexual relations until she conceived, and then shake hands and go about their merry way?

What have I gotten myself into? Just being this near to her had already wrought havoc with his senses. Now that he knew he could have this woman as his wife, his body was raring to go. Although she was above him in rank, her brother approved—nay wanted—this match.

"And what if *I* don't want a marriage of convenience?"

"Nonsense. Of course you would. You have no desire for me. I know it is my money you are interested in."

He reared back as if she'd slapped him. "That is not true."

"Oh, please. Let us not start off with lies between us. Can you honestly say you would be here arranging a marriage with me if my dowry hadn't been dangled in front of you?"

Joseph took a moment to calm himself, resisting the urge to throttle the girl. "What you say is partially true. I admit when I arrived this morning to visit with your brother, marriage to you was the furthest thing from my mind. However, since Drake has confided what happened to you recently, and offered to allow a marriage between us—if you accepted—then I will admit there are more things than money that make this arrangement appealing."

She tilted her head in question. Since he knew Abigail not to be in the least way coy, he assumed she wanted a genuine answer. Once more he took her hand in his. "You are an intelligent, vibrant, beautiful woman. Who would not want you for a wife?"

"Apparently Lord Redgrave," she said wryly.

"The man's a fool. But I am not. We've known each other since we were children. I like to think that we are already friends. A marriage between us is a first-rate idea. Of course your dowry plays into it, but I had full intentions of soliciting donations from friends here in London. Also, there is my own property, and the inheritance I will receive upon my marriage."

"What you are attempting to tell me is, if I came with no dowry, you would still entertain the idea of marrying me?"

He gave himself a minute to reflect on her question. Abigail was a woman most men would want to marry. Beautiful, smart and possessed of curves even a man of the church desired. She'd been trained to be an advantageous wife to a titled gentleman. She was graceful, witty, and gently bred. Energy radiated from her, even now making the air snap with vitality. To have all that energy in his life—and bed—would make him a fortunate man indeed. Except she was seeking to put restrictions on the bedding part of it. He sighed. Something he would need to work on. "Yes, I would."

"Then you are wrong. You *are* a fool."

"How so?"

"Because I don't want a marriage that is more than two friends working together to create something worthwhile. I held out for three years for what I thought was a love match. But apparently, that wasn't true. So now all I want is a home of my own, children, and to be needed." Though she pierced him with a determined look, her eyes rimmed with tears.

His insides tightened at the look of emptiness on her face that hadn't been there before. Since he'd always been half in love with her, placing restrictions on their relationship could prove difficult to live with. But he was not prepared to miss this chance to have Abigail as his wife. "I will honor your wishes, if that is truly what you want."

"It is."

Joseph slid off the sofa and bent to one knee, taking her hands in his. "Will you honor me then, Lady Abigail, and make me the happiest of men, by consenting to be my wife?"

At first he thought she would refuse. Then she leaned

her head to one side and said softly, "Yes, Joseph Fox. I will."

He rose and pulled her up, wrapping his arms around her waist. Bending his head to kiss her, he was once again jolted at the emotions welling up within him. Her hand slowly snaked its way up his arm until it settled on his shoulder. He cupped the back of her head and deepened the kiss, using his tongue to tease her until she allowed him to enter. After tasting the sweet nectar, he drew back. "Perhaps we should speak with your brother."

Abigail hesitated for a moment, her eyes dazed, then she seemed to pull herself together. "Yes, of course. I will have him come to us."

. . .

Abigail hurried across the room and quickly left the library, closing the door behind her. She leaned against the wall and took in a deep breath, touching her fingers to her swollen lips. Her heart was pounding as if she'd run a race. Her hands shook, and her belly did a ballet.

Hell and damnation. What have I gotten myself into?

Chapter Three

Abigail stared out the window at the rose garden cloaked in pale sunlight. Beyond her view, the dirt and smell of London on a hot summer day was a stark contrast to the peace and serenity below. The tip of her finger traced a heart on the glass, and she sighed. Her wedding day, the day of which every young girl dreams.

How different her life would now be, given the path she'd chosen. Or, more accurately, had been thrust upon her. Growing up, she'd always planned for a love match, assuming she would marry a titled gentleman and continue her life as it had always been. Country manor, London townhouse, the Season, parties, balls, musicales, the theatre.

Her love match had defected, and instead she was marrying a childhood friend. One she was deathly afraid of developing unwanted feelings for. Her life would not be one of drudgery, to be sure, but a rector's wife was not one of leisure, either. The thought energized her, filled her with excitement.

For some time now, the entire Season had become dull. She'd already spurned most of the suitable gentlemen. Each year she ached for the man who would be her true love, her life partner. She'd thought she'd found it in Redgrave, but apparently not. As much as she hated to admit it, her love hadn't quite died. Although, deep down inside she was grateful to discover the cad that he was before she married him.

Redgrave was handsome, charming and obviously a great pretender. As well as a scoundrel. On the other hand, Joseph Fox was an honorable man. Loyal and dependable, and determined to do the right thing. Qualities she'd deemed boring in previous suitors. A lesson learned.

"Abigail, you look lovely!" Her mother floated into the room in a swirl of dark blue silk.

"Thank you, Mother." She rose and closed the distance between them and took her mother's hands in hers. "Am I doing the right thing?"

"Oh, my dear. Come, let us sit."

Abigail clutched her mother's hands tightly. That still didn't stop their shaking. "Should I take this step that will change my life so?"

"You've made a wise decision. I watched Joseph grow from a small boisterous child into a kind, devoted man. He cares deeply for the people of his village and church. He will be true to you. There really isn't much more to ask for in a marriage. You get along well, and I can see the two of you working toward a goal, accomplishing a great deal."

Abigail smiled softly. "I notice you left out love."

"Because I didn't wish you to snap at me," her mother

said wryly, smoothing her skirts.

"I am determined to eschew love. I will never again put myself into a position where I can be hurt."

"Well, dearling, we've had this discussion before. In fact, so many times recently that there really isn't any more to say on the subject. Now it is time to leave for the church. Drake is waiting downstairs to escort you." She pulled Abigail into her arms in a tight hug. "Be happy, my daughter."

Several hours later, Abigail once more glanced at the wedding band on her left hand. She sat across from Joseph, who studied the scenery as their coach rumbled along toward her new home in Addysby End. She twisted the gold and emerald ring around her finger. It was done. She was now Lady Abigail Fox, wife to Rector Joseph Fox. Whether this was the right thing for her to do or not, no longer mattered. She had a new life ahead of her, and she was determined to make the best of it.

Gathering clouds cast the late afternoon into a gray pallor. They'd been on the road for a few hours, the wedding already a blur in her mind.

"Are you comfortable enough?" Joseph asked.

"Yes."

The heavy silence hung in the air. They'd already had a stilted conversation about the wedding, the food, and the change of scenery from London to the lovely countryside. Abigail was rarely at a loss for words, but no matter how hard she tried, she couldn't think of a single thing to say to her new husband. A moment of panic seized her as she thought of the possibility of years of numbing silence every time she and Joseph were alone.

They could discuss the school again, but most of the planning had been done, with not much left to consider until they spoke with the contractor who would construct the building.

She stole a glance at him under her eyelashes. At first he appeared relaxed, but after careful consideration, she realized he held himself stiffly, as if waiting for a blow. No longer able to handle the quietude, she blurted, "Will we be driving straight through?"

Startled from his musings, Joseph said, "No. There is an inn I've stayed at many times before. It is a tad more than half way from London to Addysby End. They have plain, but tasty food and comfortable beds. I'm sure the fare won't be at all what you are used to, but I'm afraid it is the best we can do."

Her eyes snapped. "I have stayed at inns before and am familiar with their offerings. I'm sure it will be fine."

The censure in her voice brought a slight flush to Joseph's face. Abigail immediately regretted her tone, but, honestly, did the man think she never traveled? And his presumption that she would somehow find the accommodations lacking vexed her. It did not bode well for this marriage if he assumed she could only survive with luxuries at her fingertips.

She leaned her head against the back of the seat and closed her eyes. The strain of the last few weeks had taken its toll. It was not like her to snap at people, and appearing to be a shrew was not how she wanted to start off their relationship.

Joseph's coach was not as luxurious as her family's

conveyance. She shifted a bit to get more comfortable.

"I'm sorry about the carriage. I do have a larger one, but generally use this one for lengthier trips. Particularly since I am almost always alone."

"It is fine." Abigail tried to tamp down her rising anger. If he said one more thing to indicate he thought her to be high in the instep and unable to bear the least amount of inconvenience, she would take off her shoe and hurl it at his head. That would certainly disabuse him of this notion that she was a princess.

She might be a duke's daughter, but she'd spent enough of her childhood running around and playing hard just like any other urchin. And if anyone should know that, it was her husband. Wasn't it he and her brother who'd tied her to a tree? She smiled at the memory. No, there was certainly nothing high in the instep about her family.

. . .

Joseph could have bitten off his tongue. What the devil was the matter with him? He knew quite well the Lacey family members did not think of themselves above everyone else. But now that he had Abigail sitting across from him, traveling to his home to begin their marriage, his brain seemed to be disconnected from his mouth.

The wedding had been quick. While they'd waited for the bride to appear, he'd tried to make small talk with his father, who stood up for him, but it hadn't worked. He still couldn't believe he was about to marry Lady Abigail. The one woman he had put firmly from his mind years ago. Despite what he'd had her believe back then, he too had felt the attraction between the two of them, but knew it could go nowhere.

But then, maybe it hadn't been so impossible. Despite being a duke, her brother had married a woman who had been raised in America and was a botanist, certainly outside the strictures of *ton* society. Penelope also still worked at her science. During the two weeks Joseph had stayed with the family, waiting for the wedding, he'd been witness to Drake following his duchess around with a shovel to do her digging, lest she fall and hurt herself. He shook his head and grinned. One only had to spend less than a half an hour in the couple's company to know they were very much in love, and devoted to each other.

Perhaps one day…He shoved that idea from his mind. Abigail had made it plain when they'd formed their original arrangement that she wanted nothing more from this union than children and the opportunity to help him with his school. As much as he wanted to see his project come to fruition, it was the begetting of children that had occupied most of his thoughts the past couple of weeks.

He slid his gaze from the gloomy exterior to his wife. Her eyes were closed, and from the peaceful expression on her face and her slightly parted lips, it was obvious she'd fallen into a deep sleep. He took the opportunity to study her closely.

While an attractive woman, her beauty actually came from her personality, her various expressions. At rest she looked lovely, but when she was awake and being Abigail, she was stunningly beautiful. Not one to be overly impressed with a woman's exterior, he was actually more fascinated by her person.

During the fleeting moments they'd been able to spend together since their betrothal, she'd questioned him relentlessly on his plans for the school. Her enthusiasm for the project stunned him, as did her suggestions. He found in his future wife a vital and energetic partner with ideas to make the design of the school much more efficient. In fact, he'd sat speechless as she'd slid paper after paper under his nose with her ideas.

But in all the times they discussed the plans and talked about various programs for the children, he'd found it hard to concentrate on her words. He'd watched her plump lips move, wanting to cover them with his own. His hands itched to feel the softness of her breasts that rose and fell with each breath. He ached to pull her onto his lap, feel her rounded bottom against his hardness.

Thinking of those conversations now had him hard, forcing him to shift in the seat to ease the discomfort.

Abigail jerked as the carriage hit a bump in the road. She blinked a few times as if confused, then her brows furrowed as she looked out the small window. She swung her gaze to him and a combination of confusion and mirth slid across her face as she clutched the strap in the carriage. "Bumpy ride."

"If you prefer, you can sit alongside me, and I'll hold onto you."

She shook her head. "I'm fine over here. How long was I asleep?"

"Not long. Only about fifteen minutes."

She stretched her muscles. "Do you mind if I read?"

"Not at all. I've a book myself." With dusk encroaching, he reached up and lit the lantern hanging alongside him, casting the space into a cozy niche.

She reached into a small bag at her feet and withdrew a book. Opening to a page marked with a small card, she began to read.

Joseph opened his book, but instead of reading, he watched her from under half-closed eyelids, observing her staring at the same page for over five minutes. Then he grinned at the fact that she held the book upside down.

Suddenly the carriage hit a large hole in the road. "Oh!" Abigail's book flew from her hands, and she landed on the floor, her skirts up around her knees. She glanced up at him, her face a bright red as she shoved her skirts down.

Joseph reached for her and pulled her up alongside him. Abigail swatted at his hands when he tried to right her jacket. "I'm fine." She smoothed her hair back, and scooted once more to the other side of the carriage, her forgotten tome still at her feet. "Do you suppose we might stop for tea?"

"Of course." He didn't know whether to be amused or hurt that she was so quick to bat his hand away. Did she expect that he would never touch her?

He tapped on the ceiling of the carriage as a signal to the driver to stop at the next posting inn.

As it turned out, it was the inn where Joseph had planned to stop for the evening. He checked his timepiece. "It seems we will be partaking of dinner instead of tea."

"Goodness. Is it that late already?"

"Almost seven."

"It will be good to be free of the coach and ease my muscles."

The footman opened the door, and Joseph jumped out,

turning to assist Abigail. The warmth of her hand in his once more brought his attention to what lay ahead of them. His wedding night.

"Mr. Fox, how nice to see you again." The innkeeper greeted them as they entered the main room.

"And you as well, Weston." Joseph pulled Abigail forward. "I'm pleased to inform you I've recently married, and this is my wife, Lady Abigail Fox."

The man immediately bowed and pulled on his forelock. "Milady."

Abigail smiled in return before the innkeeper nodded to Joseph. "May I congratulate you on your marriage and your lovely bride?"

"Thank you. May we have a private dining room?"

"Of course. My wife will be happy to assist your lady to refresh herself." He led them through the common dining area to a small room at the back. Even though it was early summer, a fire burned, keeping the night dampness from the room.

"Please excuse me, I will send in Mrs. Weston."

Abigail moved toward the fireplace extending her hands. Within minutes, the innkeeper's wife arrived and escorted her to the privy.

The two women departed, and Joseph tamped down the nervous twitches in his stomach. He wanted everything to be perfect for her. There was no doubt any feelings Abigail had for him stemmed from their childhood. If in the future, she ever felt anything more, he would consider it a blessing. To have her for his wife was beyond anything of which he'd ever dreamed. As much as he'd like to beat Redgrave to a pulp for what he'd done to Abigail, he should send the man a thank you note. Abigail was now his.

Abigail returned to the private dining room the same time the innkeeper was delivering a drink to Joseph.

"I asked for tea to be sent." He said as he held her chair.

"Thank you. I think I need that more than I do food, at this point." She studied him for a moment. "Joseph, may I ask you something?"

"Of course."

"You have known me and my family for many years."

He nodded as he took a sip of his brandy. Once again he was having a difficult time concentrating on her words. All he saw where those plump, ripe lips moving. His groin tightened as his thoughts drifted toward the bedrooms upstairs where he soon would be alone with his wife to nibble on those soft lips, and then proceed south from there...

"You must remember my mother organizing games for the village children. Do you recall how she used to rescue puppies and lead us all in snowball fights?"

He pulled himself back from his lascivious thoughts and replayed her question in his mind, grinning at the picture of the dowager duchess behaving in a most un-duchess like manner many times over the years. It was one of the reasons he'd always been so comfortable at Manchester Manor. Never did anyone make him feel as though he was beneath them and had no right to be there. He and Drake had been friends throughout their childhood.

Abigail nodded her thanks to the innkeeper who placed a tea pot, cup and saucer in front of her.

Before she was able to pick up the conversation again, the innkeeper's wife arrived with bowls of fragrant stew, warm fresh bread and butter. Her stomach gave a very unladylike growl as the enticing smells wafted in the air. "Oh, this looks wonderful!"

Mrs. Weston blushed as she placed a dish of steaming vegetables on the table. "Thank you, milady."

Once the innkeeper and his wife withdrew from the room, Abigail tasted her stew and murmured her delight. "This is delicious."

Those rich lips covered her spoon in a way that had his mouth drying up. He cleared his throat, pulling his gaze way from the sight. "I've always found their fare to be tasty. But simple."

"That is what I want to speak with you about." Abigail placed her spoon alongside her bowl. "Joseph, you know the sort of family I come from, and that my brother married a woman who most of the *ton* perceived as unsuitable."

"Now, wait just a minute. Her Grace is a wonderful—"

"I know, I know." She waved her hand. "I was not disparaging my sister-in-law. In fact, I love her dearly and am thrilled beyond imagining she is a part of my family. I merely wanted to point that out to you, because I get the feeling you assume whatever life you enjoy, and have offered to me, is somehow lacking. That I will be unhappy married to a rector."

"That is not exactly true—"

"Yes, it is. You keep apologizing. For your coach, the inn, the food. Heavens, have I ever given you the impression that I needed luxury to survive?"

Joseph used his index finger to draw around the rim of his glass, avoiding her gaze. "No. Neither you, nor any member of your family has ever given me that impression. I apologize. You no doubt think I am an idiot."

"No. That isn't what I think. I just wanted to get that out of the way. It was beginning to feel awkward."

He reached across the table and took her hand. "I'm sorry. I didn't mean to make you uncomfortable."

"I know."

Abigail slid her hand out from under his and continued with her meal. Once she finished, she wiped her mouth, and carefully laid the serviette next to her plate. Taking in a deep breath, she said, "There is also one more thing I would like to address."

"Yes?"

A slight blush began on her neck above the lace on her bodice. It slowly spread to her face as she fiddled with her spoon, swallowing several times. She glanced at him, then back down again, extremely interested in the pattern on the plate holding a piece of bread. Her fingers began to crumble the bread as she worked her mouth, apparently having a problem forming whatever words she intended to speak.

What the devil was the problem now? She definitely looked decidedly uneasy.

Abigail blurted, "I don't wish to consummate our marriage just yet."

Chapter Four

Joseph swallowed his drink and was overtaken by a paroxysm of coughing. He didn't believe he'd heard correctly. Did his new wife just tell him she had no desire to join him in bed on their wedding night? Based on her red face and the nervous fumbling she was doing with her spoon, he had a sinking feeling that was exactly what she'd just said. But this was Abigail! The most outspoken, strong and independent of the Lacey girls. She'd never been a bashful miss, and there certainly was nothing shy or retiring about her.

Then it struck him. She was still in love with Redgrave. After all the man had done to her. Despite the disgrace and humiliation, her feelings for the cad were still so strong she could not give herself to her husband. The hurt at her rejection was swiftly shoved aside as anger took over.

"As you wish, madam. Far be it from me to force my own wife to my bed."

Abigail's head jerked up, and she stared at him wide-eyed. She stiffened and nodded. "Very well, then."

"That is your desire—I mean, your preference?"

"Yes. Indeed. I would like to wait."

"For what?"

"Well. Until I feel—you know—until such time that it seems...appropriate." She finished lamely.

His eyebrows rose. "Appropriate? We are married."

"I know that, but it was all so sudden."

Sudden? They'd known each other since she was out of leading strings. His gut tightened when he wondered if she would have given this ultimatum to Redgrave. Before his brain could take control of his mouth, the words were out. "Is that the arrangement you had with Redgrave?"

Abigail paled and gasped. "No. That is, we never discussed it."

He leaned forward. "Why did you not discuss it?"

"It never came up, and besides we were betrothed for a few months. So we were more familiar."

"Familiar? My dear wife, I have seen you with your undergarments plastered to your body as you came out of the lake after swimming with your sisters."

"I was eleven years old!"

Joseph downed the rest of his brandy and called for more. He slid his empty bowl away from him as the innkeeper brought a bottle and placed it on the table.

"When you are ready to retire, Mr. Fox, my wife has a special room prepared for you and your new wife."

Joseph grunted as he poured the brandy into his glass.

"Thank you, Weston," Abigail said. "If your wife will be so kind as to show me to our room, I am ready to retire."

Joseph muttered under his breath, then swilled the

brown liquid in his glass. It was just as well he'd learned that Abigail's feelings were still engaged. She'd been right. Their marriage was no more than an arrangement for two people to work together to build the school, attend to the needs of his parishioners, and produce children. Although the producing of children would be a tad difficult if she did not want to share his bed.

"I will see you upstairs." Abigail slid back her chair as the innkeeper's wife entered the room.

Joseph saluted her with his glass and downed the drink. He knew he was behaving like an arse, but he was angry. It stung to be newly married and discover that your wife was in love with another man.

• • •

Abigail stiffened her spine and left the room, trailing behind the portly woman who led her upstairs. If she ever needed proof that the only reason Joseph had married her was because of her dowry, his attitude when she said she didn't want to consummate their marriage just yet, confirmed it.

He had not even tried to dissuade her, only questioned her on Redgrave. Whatever had he to do with the conversation? Joseph hadn't even asked her to explain. Not that she could have, since she had no idea why she'd said what she had. As she'd sat at the table with a new husband, with the night looming in front of her, she'd felt uneasy, as if she were doing something wrong. So in a fit of panic, she'd made that stupid statement.

Instead of the blasted man attempting to deter her from her decision by sweet talking, or even trying to seduce her, he'd brought Redgrave into the discussion. Then he'd merely accepted her words and proceeded to attempt to drink the inn dry.

After bidding the innkeeper's wife a good night, she mumbled to herself as she set her bonnet and gloves on the dresser. She didn't want sweet talking, bald-faced lies, and false romance, anyway. She'd got precisely what she'd wanted. A marriage that would provide her with a home and, eventually, children. And an outlet for her energy. If that didn't sit well, then she'd not spend a great deal of time wallowing in self-pity.

As she unbuttoned her pelisse, she surveyed the room. By public inn standards, it was lovely. Someone had turned down the bed sheets and lit candles around the room. A bottle of wine rested in a bucket, along with two wine glasses. Her eyes took that all in, but settled on the large tub near the fireplace with steam rising from the water.

A bath would be just the thing. Once the promised maid arrived, Abigail would soak in the hot water until her skin wrinkled.

Much later, she wandered the room in her nightgown, examining the bottle of wine, tempted to open it and have a glass, then set it firmly down in the bucket.

Hell and damnation, where was the man? Was he so annoyed with her that he planned to sleep at the dining table? She'd no sooner formed that complete thought when there was a banging on the room door.

"Yes?"

"Open the door."

The voice sounded like Joseph, but odd, and his words a bit garbled. She hurried to the door. "Joseph? Is that you?"

"I think so," he answered sotto voce.

Frowning, she opened the door. Joseph had apparently been leaning against it, and the movement caused him to bolt into the room. Arms spinning, he fought to keep himself upright as he barreled past her.

He stumbled to the bed, grabbed the bedpost and hung on, swinging to and fro. "I am here."

Her eyebrows rose. "Indeed."

He pulled himself up and released the bedpost, only to make a grab for it when he started to slide sideways.

"Sir, you are drunk!"

"I believe you are right, wife." He hiccupped.

His hair stood straight up, as if he'd spent the past few hours running his fingers through it. His coat was gone, his cravat hung limply around his neck. He peered at her through blood shot eyes. "I am sorry there is only one bed. At least I think there is only one. Right now it is hard to say. It appears we will be forced to sleep next to each other, or I can sleep on the floor." He burped.

Abigail wasn't altogether sure that was what he said, his words coming out somewhat twisted. As he released one hand from the bedpost to wave at the bed, then at the floor, it was her best guess.

"There is no need for you to sleep on the floor. I can sleep in the chair."

He shook his head, then moaned. "No, should not do that," he mumbled. "Not gentlemanly."

"What?"

"Nothing. You will not sleep in the chair." He surrendered his battle to remain upright, and sat on the bed, swaying, trying hard to focus on her. "Stand still."

Abigail sighed. She'd seen her brother in his cups a few times, so she knew there was no point in attempting a conversation. She strode to the bed and poked him in his chest. As she expected, he fell backward. Kneeling, she tugged his boots off, then stood, hands on her hips and regarded him. He was already snoring.

She shook her head in disgust as she moved around the room, blowing out what was left of the candles. With the pale moonlight filtering in through the window, she climbed into bed, and pulled up the blanket. She lay on her back, her hands clasped on her stomach.

No doubt she'd made a mistake in asking for time before they made love. On the other hand, in doing so, she'd learned what prompted Joseph to marry her. And it was certainly not any great desire to take her to bed. She thumped the pillow and turned onto her stomach. It didn't matter. As long as they were intimate enough times for her to conceive a child, she would be happy.

Or at least content.

• • •

Abigail shifted, snuggling closer to the warmth. There was a thumping in her ear, the soothing cadence almost lulling her back to sleep until she became aware of her surroundings. She was lying in bed, but she was not alone. She moved her fingers and the tips came into contact with warm skin.

Her knee was bent, but also lying atop warm skin. Warm and hairy. A leg. Goodness gracious, a man's leg. *Joseph!* She slowly moved her head, tilting her chin until she looked into two deep brown eyes staring back at her. "Oh."

She was sprawled all over her husband's body in a most unladylike fashion. Her husband's naked body! She scooted back, immediately feeling bereft at the loss of warmth. "Why are you undressed?"

"Because I sleep that way."

"But you were dressed last night. All I did was remove your boots."

"Yes, well I awoke a few hours ago and divested myself of my clothing." He extended his hand. "Come here, Abigail."

She shook her head, pulling the covers up to her chin. Joseph slid closer, tracing circles on her cheek with his finger. "So soft." He cupped her face, rubbing his thumb along her lips.

Heat began to rise in her middle, spreading upward, causing tingles in her breasts. Was he preparing to do now what she'd denied him last night? Perhaps it would be best to get it over with, so she wouldn't have to worry about it all day.

His warm fingers traced her jawline, moving down to her throat, where they circled, then lower to her chest, to the top of her breasts. Her breathing hitched, and she waited for what he would do next.

She licked her lips and dragged her gaze from the mesmerizing sight of his fingers to his face. His brown eyes had darkened to almost black, his eyelids heavy. He wrapped his palm around her neck and tugged her toward him.

Abigail began to move forward, then jerked back and quickly rolled over, away from him, her feet landing squarely on the floor. "I need to clean my mouth."

His unamused chuckle followed her as she hurried to the wash bowl sitting on the dresser across the room. She eyed him in the mirror, leaning against the pillows, his hands tucked behind his head as he watched her. He was devastatingly handsome with his tumbled hair resting on his forehead, a slight smile teasing his lips. His bare chest was more muscular than she would have thought a rector's chest ought to be. Light brown hairs dusted the center area, snaking down to disappear under the blanket at his waist.

A distinct bulge raised the sheet over his lap. When he noticed her staring at that spot, he grinned. Flustered, she drew her eyes away and did a quick wash of her face and hands, and brushed her teeth. She grabbed her frock and under things and bolted behind the dressing screen. Within seconds she heard Joseph leave the bed, and rustling sounds that indicated he was dressing.

Her flesh burned as she slid the nightgown off and wiggled into her chemise. She placed her hands on her cheeks, trying to dismiss what had just happened. Already her determination to hold herself apart from him was in jeopardy. The man had barely touched her, and even now she had to fight to keep from whipping her chemise off and dragging him back to the bed to finish what he'd started.

With a deep breath, she pulled herself together to continue dressing. She would not allow him to fluster her, to cause her to shilly-shally about how this marriage would go on. They had work to do, and allowing whatever it was he'd just done to her get in the way, would destroy her resolve.

Holding out her stays, she considered the problem of how to lace them up. Either she could leave them off—as no lady would do—or ask her husband to help. "Joseph?"

"Yes." From the sound of his voice and the splashing, she assumed he was at the wash bowl.

"Can you, er, that is, would you be so kind as to—"

"What?"

"I need help with my stays." Once again her face heated as though she would burst into flames. What was the matter with her? She had never been shy or hesitant. It appeared marriage had turned her into a blathering idiot.

"Certainly. Come out here where I can see better."

Clutching the garment to her chest, she stepped out from behind the dressing screen and presented her back to him. Whereupon her husband—the rector—proceeded to lace her up with all the speed and experience that she would have expected from a London rake. A bit disconcerted by that, she returned to finish dressing.

"I will go downstairs and arrange for our breakfast," Joseph said.

"Thank you. I shall join you shortly."

She exhaled when she heard the door close. This would not do. She was a nervous wreck, and she had no idea why. This was Joseph, for heaven's sake. She'd known him all her life. He had been her first infatuation, her brother's best friend. Why should she be so uncomfortable with him now that they were alone?

Perhaps it was best if she didn't try to answer that question.

• • •

Joseph studied Abigail's profile as their carriage drew closer to Addsby End. Earlier, when he'd awoken and realized his wife was sprawled all over him, his morning erection had grown to an agonizing size. Her soft breasts beneath her thin nightgown were tucked into his side, her pointed nipples prickling his skin.

Curly hairs that had escaped the braid she'd fastened lay against her silky skin, moving up and down as she took in and let out air. Her plump lips were slightly parted, glistening in the morning light. He had called on all of his control to keep from bending his head and kissing those berry-colored temptations.

Although the conversation held steady as they rode toward home, neither of them brought up her request last night, nor the position she'd found herself in this morning. He laughed to himself. For a woman who all of a sudden had developed maidenly concerns, she'd certainly seemed quite comfortable draped all over him.

They rounded the bend in the road, and the village appeared, once again filling him with a sense of familiar comfort, and gladness that his time in London was over. If he had his way, he would never leave Addysby End. Another concern with having Abigail as a wife. Raised with the attractions, shopping, and entertainments of London, would she be satisfied with life here?

"Oh, this is lovely, Joseph," Abigail whispered, almost reverently, gazing out the small window. "So many times I promised myself I would ride to your village since it is only a half day from Manchester Manor, but I never seemed to take the time. I can't believe how much I missed." She turned to him. "It is beautiful."

Warmth spread through him at her admiration. The snug town was built into the side of a hill, stretching out to the valley. A low stone wall surrounded the village part of the area, with the emerald green hillside dotted with sheep, goats and cows. A large space was enclosed by a wooden fence where about twenty horses grazed.

"Do you think you will be happy here? Away from the excitement and bustle of London?"

Abigail turned toward him, a sad smile on her face. "After three Seasons, London had already become tiresome. In fact, I had suggested to Redgrave that once we were married we cut the Season short and return to his country manor."

"And?"

She shrugged. "He didn't want to leave Town. Said he had too many obligations there. I guess I know now what those *obligations* were."

Joseph reached across the space and took her hand in his. "Please try to put that all behind you. The man is a worthless cur."

"Oh, look. Someone's pig got loose!" Abigail giggled as they watched two young boys attempting to capture the animal, which was having none of it.

"That's John and Matthew Dinger," Joseph said. "The Dinger family has five children, most of them more than ready to start school."

"Oh, dear." Abigail's hand flew to cover her mouth.

Running down the road, apparently attempting to help her big brothers, little Agnes Dinger, no more than perhaps three years, joined the chase. As they watched, the pig stopped and snorted. He turned and started back toward the little girl, who came to a halt, wide-eyed, her feet seeming to be frozen to the ground.

Joseph tapped on the ceiling of the carriage to notify the driver to a stop. He flung open the door, both he and Abigail jumping out. "Get back inside," he shouted at her.

Ignoring his command, she sped to the left of the road, while Joseph took the right side. The pig continued to give chase, and finally the little girl spun on her little legs and ran toward her house. But the pig was faster.

Joseph began shouting and waving at the pig, trying to chase him in another direction, but he continued on his path toward Agnes. He picked up a few stones and tossed them, but the animal ignored them, focused as he was on his prize.

Agnes spotted Abigail and turned, her chubby legs trying very hard to run to her. Joseph continued to call out to the pig, casting a few more pebbles. The brothers were getting closer to catching the animal, but the beast was too close to Agnes for Joseph's liking.

Abigail sped up, reached the little girl, and scooped her into her arms. Joseph's heart almost stopped when the pig crashed into Abigail's legs, sending both her and Agnes sprawling on the ground. Then in the way of animals, the pig stopped, grunted a few times and wandered away.

"Abigail!" Joseph was nearly out of breath when he reached her side. Agnes was crying, her little face scrunched up.

Joseph pulled Agnes from Abigail's arms, then after giving her a quick once over, handed her off to her brother. He dropped to his knees and turned Abigail over. "Are you all right?"

Her face revealed numerous marks where gravel from the pathway had scraped her skin. "I'm fine. How is the little girl?"

"You are not fine. Your face is all scratched up. I told you to return to the carriage."

She groaned as she started to stand.

"Agnes is fine. Well, she's a little frightened, but her brothers took her home."

"And the pig?"

Joseph helped her up, clutching her to his side as her steps faltered. "The pig decided to return home as well."

Abigail stumbled again, and Joseph lifted her into his arms and headed to the carriage.

"For heaven's sake, put me down. I can walk."

"You do not follow instructions well. I told you to go back into the carriage."

"And if I had, the little girl might have been hurt."

"Nonsense. Between me and her brothers we would have rescued her."

Abigail crossed her arms over her chest and snorted. "Hardly. I was the closest to her."

Joseph climbed into the carriage, still holding Abigail to his chest. He signaled to the drive to start up, and they continued on their way. He shifted Abigail and removed a handkerchief from his pocket. Gently, he started to clear away the stones from her cheeks.

Now that his heart had return to its normal rhythm, he wanted to throttle her. Beyond her scraped face, the way she winced when he shifted her told him she apparently suffered some type of injury. "I will send for the physician when we arrive home."

Abigail sighed. "I don't need a physician, I'm just a bit scratched up."

He glared at her and continued his ministrations until the carriage pulled up in front of his home. As soon as the footman had the door opened, he climbed out still clutching

Abigail and headed toward the door that was immediately opened by his housekeeper, Mrs. O'Neill.

She grasped her throat, her eyes wide. "My goodness. Who have we here, Mr. Fox?"

"Who we have here, Mrs. O'Neill, is my wife."

"Your wife? I thought you were going to London to find donors for your school."

"Er, I got a bit sidetracked. It is a long story. But right now my wife has been injured in a fall, and I would like you to send for a physician."

"I don't need a physician." Abigail shifted in Joseph's arms and turned to the woman. "I am pleased to meet you, Mrs. O'Neill. I am Lady Abigail Fox, and am I to assume you are the housekeeper?"

Mrs. O'Neill bobbed a curtsey, her demeanor quickly changing to one of awe. "Yes, my lady. I see your lovely face is all scraped up. Please let me send for a physician."

"She also seems to have hurt her . . . well, other places." He mumbled this last bit, his cheeks heating.

• • •

Abigail fumed at the position Joseph had put her into. Here she was, the lady of the house, meeting the housekeeper for the first time, being carried into her new home like an invalid. She turned to ask once again to be put down and winced at the pain in her hip. When she'd been knocked to the ground by the pig, she'd twisted her body to keep from landing on the little girl. In doing so, she'd went down hard on her hip, then her head had slammed into the ground, whacking her cheek.

She'd only gotten a quick look at the outside of Joseph's house. Well, actually, her house as well. A stone structure, with a slated roof, it was much larger than she'd expected. Given the amount of windows, there must be more than twenty bed chambers.

Joseph hurried up the stairs, striding down the hall to a room at the very end of the corridor. Mrs. O'Neill quickly opened the door and they entered.

The room was very masculine, with no frills or feminine touches. A large poster bed in the middle of the room was made up in a dark green counterpane. Matching drapes hung on the generous windows. Everything was neat and tidy. Abigail breathed deeply, and the familiar scent of sandalwood, leather, and Joseph drifted to her nostrils.

Joseph laid her gently on the bed. "Mrs. O'Neill, would you be so good as to assist Lady Abigail out of her clothes and into a nightgown? I will see about having the physician come and take a look at her."

Abigail was mortified. What a horrible beginning to her introduction to Joseph's home and staff.

"I will be happy to help you, my lady." Mrs. O'Neill shooed Joseph toward the door. "Hurry and see about the doctor for your lady, and I'll have her all cleaned up and in bed before you return."

"I really don't need to be in bed. Aside from a few scratches I feel fine." Abigail winced again as she attempted to stand.

"Is that right?" Joseph glared at her. "You may have broken something, and you will stay in bed until you have been examined." He strode from the room, then turned as he gripped the latch. "Mrs. O'Neill, you have my permission to tie my wife to the bed in order to keep her there."

"Oh!" Abigail gritted her teeth. Her upbringing refused to allow her to show any more anger than that in front of the housekeeper. But when she got Mr. Joseph Fox alone, she would certainly give him a piece of her mind.

Tie me to the bed, indeed!

Chapter Five

The next morning after sleeping away the previous afternoon and evening, restlessness urged Abigail to insist on getting out of bed. The scratches on her face were healing, thanks to the salve Mrs. O'Neill had given her. The physician had pronounced her fit, with no broken bones. He'd given her laudanum to ease the pain in her hip. Despite the soreness in her body, she wanted to explore her new home.

She vaguely remembered Joseph coming into the room sometime last evening. He'd touched her gently on her cheek, bent to kiss her on the forehead, but then he had taken his leave. She wasn't sure where he'd slept. Or even if the room she was now in was to be hers permanently.

A bit bereft at the thought of them sharing separate bedrooms, she chided herself for her self-pity. It had been her idea to postpone the marriage bed for a while. Of course, now that she was sorry she'd done that, her pride kept her from approaching Joseph on the matter.

After receiving direction from the maid who'd attended her, Abigail made her way down the stairs to the breakfast room. Once more she was impressed with the house. The breakfast room's walls were papered in yellow and white striped silk. The floor to ceiling windows let in sufficient light, despite the gloomy day.

Joseph sat at the table, and immediately came to his feet when she entered. "How are you feeling?"

"A bit sore, truth be told, but I didn't want to lay about in bed any longer."

He touched her cheek lightly where the scratches had already begun to heal. "I would prefer if you stayed abed at least one more day."

"Nonsense. I need to work these muscles to keep from becoming stiff."

She took the seat alongside him. Breakfast was apparently informally served, with platters of eggs, bacon, and biscuits in the center of the table. There was also a plate of kippers in a cream sauce and a large bowl of fruit.

"Tea?" Joseph asked

"Please." She moved her cup forward so he could pour her tea. "Don't you drink tea?" Abigail asked noting the darker liquid in his cup.

"No. I prefer coffee in the morning."

Abigail made a face. The few times she'd tried the beverage it had struck her as bitter. She added some eggs and toast to her plate, along with an orange. "You've an orangery?"

Joseph looked up from the newspaper he'd been reading. "Yes. It came with the property when I purchased it."

"I must admit I'm a bit surprised at the size of your

home."

"Our home." He smiled at her blush.

"Our home." She began to peel the orange. "I thought you were in London to raise money for your school?"

Joseph pushed away his empty plate and drew his coffee cup closer. "I am sure you know my grandfather was the Earl of Hornsforth. His wife—my grandmother—had various properties in her own name. She left me two of them, along with a trust from which I receive the yearly income until I reach the age of five and thirty—or marry—and then it becomes mine in its entirety."

"How strange."

"Not really. She never approved of me going into the church, even though my father is also a rector. I think she was reconciled to his calling because he was her second son, whereas I am my father's only child. I think she hoped I would eventually change my mind and use the money to help secure a seat in the House of Commons."

"And she assumed having a wife would steer you toward a political career?"

"So it would seem, but I love my work with my parishioners. I don't want to go anywhere near Parliament."

Apparently Joseph had not only received her dowry to use for his school, but his own funds would be released upon his marriage. The reason for him agreeing to wed became more obvious every day. Even though her own motives were less than noble, a slight feeling of sadness filled her. Then she gave herself a shake. This was precisely what she'd wanted. A marriage with nothing more than an understanding between them. No foolishness like love to cause strife.

"After seeing some of the machinations that Drake

has to go through in the House of Lords, I cannot say that I blame you." She took a sip of her tea. "Where are your other properties?"

"I sold one of them, which allowed me to purchase this house. The other is in Cornwall. There is a very competent steward who runs the place."

"Do you ever visit?"

"About twice a year."

"How very interesting. I should enjoy going with you the next time you make the trip."

"Of course. I am sure the tenants would love to meet you."

Abigail returned to her breakfast. She'd suffered one surprise after another since their wedding. Joseph was not the sober, sanctimonious man she'd assumed. It still rankled at how quickly he'd laced her up at the inn. He also maintained a very comfortable life, with numerous staff. Somehow, she'd expected her life to be, while not exactly poor, at least not quite as opulent as it appeared. But on the other hand, Drake would have made certain she would be amply provided for.

"I think perhaps after breakfast we might take a stroll around the garden," Joseph said.

"I would like that." She glanced out the window. "We had best make it right after breakfast. It appears we may be in for some rain."

"After our stroll, I will have Mrs. O'Neill introduce you to the staff."

Abigail was about to question him on the sleeping arrangements when the butler she'd met yesterday stepped into the breakfast room. "Sir, you have a caller."

"So early, Manning? Who is here?"

"Lady Durham has arrived."

Joseph shoved back his chair, a smile on his lips. "Send her in." He turned to Abigail. "Lady Durham is widowed and a member of the parish. She has helped a great deal with church projects and is especially excited about the new school."

"Mr. Fox!" Lady Durham glided into the room, holding out her hands. Their visitor was another addition to Abigail's list of surprises. Expecting to see an older, somewhat stocky woman who was devoting her life to the church, Abigail was stunned to see an absolutely beautiful young lady. Not much older than Abigail, Lady Durham was dressed in the height of fashion in a lavender muslin gown, with purple embroidery around the bodice. Her red hair was smoothed back from her face. Her black and lavender bonnet framed a sweet countenance. Except for her eyes, which implied a cold and calculating mind. Despite this woman's soft and friendly demeanor, Abigail shivered.

"Lady Durham, how nice to see you." Joseph took her hand in his and raised it to his lips.

She patted his cheek warmly.

She's a bit forward.

"I just couldn't wait to hear how successful you were in London. You were gone much longer than I expected." Lady Durham took the seat Joseph held out for her, glancing in Abigail's direction, her eyebrows raised apparently in surprise. "And may I be made known to your guest?"

Joseph took his seat and placed his hand over Abigail's. "Lady Durham, I would like you to meet my wife, Lady Abigail Fox."

The woman took in a deep breath, and her face turned as pale as new snow. Her eyes darted back and forth between Abigail and Joseph, her nostrils flaring with…what? Anger? Surprise?

"Your wife?" her voice trilled, actually hurting Abigail's ears. Swallowing rapidly, she added, "Surely you are joking, Mr. Fox." She lowered her voice to almost a whisper.

A confused smile on his face, he shook his head. "Not at all. I assure you, Lady Durham, this is no joke. Lady Abigail and I were wed in London three days ago. I'm hoping once you become better acquainted, you will be good friends."

"How do you do, Lady Durham? I am pleased to meet you." Abigail attempted to put the woman at ease, since she'd notably been taken aback by Joseph's announcement.

Lady Durham merely nodded briefly. The silence that followed became almost painful as the woman fussed with the sleeves of her dress. Joseph cleared his throat a few times, apparently lost as to what exactly had just happened at his breakfast table.

Abigail wondered if perhaps Lady Durham had had intentions toward her husband. But from the look on Joseph's face, the thought had never crossed his mind.

"Would you care for tea?" Abigail said, smiling pleasantly at their guest.

"No, thank you. In fact, I'm afraid I must run off. I just now remembered an appointment." She rose quickly and headed for the door, almost crashing into Joseph as he jumped up to pull out her chair. With a quick wave, she left the room, her hurried footsteps echoing in the hall until the sound of the door closing left them in stunned silence.

"That was strange." Joseph continued to stare at the

closed door.

. . .

Lady Edith Durham breezed by Manning, her insides quaking with anger. How dare Joseph return from London with a wife! That was to be her role. She'd spent numerous hours at the blasted church, attempting to gain Joseph's favor. Her year of mourning was almost up, and she had decided to make known her intentions very soon. All her planning and plotting had come to naught.

So caught up in her internal reverie, she hadn't even noticed where she had ended up. She'd also forgotten that she'd arrived in her coach. The devil take the man for distracting her so! She reversed her course, and headed back to the ninny driver who had seen her stomp away from the house, but never thought to follow her. If she wasn't paying him such a low wage, she'd fire the dolt.

"Take me home," she grumbled as she slapped at the footman who held his hand out to help her into the carriage.

Damn, damn, damn. Just the thought of the tidy income Joseph enjoyed, along with the money from his trust, made her eyes water at the loss.

Men. They were the bane of her existence. She'd thought when she escaped from the brutal clutches of her father that she would never have to worry about the vile creatures again. Except she'd soon discovered that a woman alone was a target for every sort of blackguard on God's good earth.

After two years of being pinched, patted, and grabbed while she attempted to serve drinks at a tavern, she'd bought some fashionable clothes from her meager savings and headed to London. With fake references, she began work at a dress shop, and by mimicking the accents of the ladies who had come into the shop, she'd secured a position as a companion to the former Lady Durham.

Thankfully, the old Lord Durham hadn't been too particular about who he hired as a companion to his wife. Within weeks, the woman had died, and Edith had been right there, ready to take her place. Who would have guessed that the old Earl was busy running his estate into the ground, so when he turned up his toes, all Edith had inherited was a small income that barely kept her alive?

When the new Lord Durham had arrived to claim his inheritance, he hadn't been the least bit taken with her attempts at seduction. She'd been quickly removed before he'd installed his insipid wife and three brats.

She'd be damned if she was going to lose this latest opportunity, with no other promising quarry in this benighted town. No matter what, she would not go back to being poor again. Something had to be done about this *wife* of his. Something permanent, that would remove greedy Lady Abigail's hands from money that should have been hers.

Tomorrow, when she wasn't seething from anger and could think clearly, she'd come up with an idea.

Bloody hell.

• • •

Abigail tapped lightly on the housekeeper's sitting room door.

"Come in," the woman said.

"Good afternoon, Mrs. O'Neill."

"Oh, my lady. Please have a seat." The housekeeper flushed and jumped up from where she sat, writing in a ledger.

"Thank you." Abigail perched on the edge of one of the comfortable chairs in the room and adjusted her skirts. She smiled in the older woman's direction. "I thought you might give me a tour of the house and introduce me to the staff. That is, if this is a good time for you."

"Any time you wish, my lady. May I send for some tea before we start?"

"No, thank you. I just finished luncheon, and Mr. Fox is out of the house, meeting with the contractor for the school building. I would prefer to start on the tour, if it is all the same to you."

"Of course." Mrs. O'Neill closed the ledger. "Do you wish to see the kitchen?"

"Yes. Please. I'd like to see the entire house."

"Very well, then. That is where we will start."

The wonderful smells coming from the kitchen greeted them long before they entered the room. After being introduced to Cook, who in turned introduced her to the assistants, they made their way to the servant's eating area, and then to the larder.

Except for the smaller size of Joseph's house compared to Manchester Manor, things seemed to be run very much like her childhood home. Everywhere they went, Abigail saw efficiency, and cheerful, hard-working servants. Each one she'd been introduced to was polite and spoke of Joseph in a caring and respectful manner. He apparently enjoyed a great deal of regard from his staff, which was really no surprise, given everything she already knew about her husband.

"This room has not been used since Mr. Fox moved in, because until recently, there was no Mrs. Fox," Mrs. O'Neill said as she threw open the door to the master suite.

"Were you here then when Mr. Fox bought the house?"

"Yes. Most of the staff came along with the purchase, as the prior owner, Lady Wentworth, sold it and moved to Lancashire to reside with her eldest daughter." She lowered her voice, as if the woman could hear her miles away. "Lady Wentworth had grown somewhat forgetful, and her daughter, Mrs. Brightmore, insisted she move into her home."

They'd entered into the suite through the sitting room door, which connected the two bed chambers. Abigail was startled to realize she'd been brought to Joseph's bed chamber yesterday, and had spent the night there. When she'd awakened this morning, she hadn't paid much attention once the maid had arrived to help her dress.

Married couples of her station did not generally share the same bed for sleeping purposes, although her parents had done so all the years her father had been alive. Her brother and his wife had also adopted their parents' habit. She would have to speak with Joseph soon about the sleeping arrangements. Did he intend for them to share the same bed?

"Of course, I am sure Mr. Fox will want you to decorate your bed chamber whatever way you wish, my lady."

Mrs. O'Neill had been speaking while Abigail pondered her husband's preferences regarding where she would lay her head each night. "Yes, well . . . I will speak with him about that."

As they continued the tour, Abigail listened with half an ear, caught up with thoughts of the future of her marriage. Soon she and Joseph would have to speak seriously on some issues. What exactly did he want from this marriage?

Because of her dowry and his trust fund, he now had all the money necessary to build the school, hire a teacher, and buy supplies.

Lack of cooperation by the parents was one of the pitfalls of schools for the lower classes. Most schools run by churches charged a penny a day for each student. When a parent didn't have the penny, the child couldn't get a lesson that day. By Joseph funding the school on his own, that obstacle to education had been removed.

What would be her place in their life? She would love to teach. She grew excited at the idea of instructing the children how to read and to write with a clear hand. It would be important for the boys to learn how to add and subtract, and the girls how to sew a neat seam. Since most of the parents in the parish worked hard each day to keep food on the table, there wasn't time to see to a child's education. That would be her place.

Their tour came to an end at the same time Abigail decided to seek out Joseph so they could make some plans. Her life had taken an abrupt turn by marrying a rector. Days filled with helping people live a better life would replace visits to the *modiste,* musicales, balls, and parties.

She couldn't wait to start her new life.

Chapter Six

Joseph stood at the front of the assembly room and rapped on the table with a gavel. "My friends, may I have your attention, please? If you would take your seats, we can start."

Abigail sat at the head table, feeling a tad uncomfortable as murmurs crested over the group like an ocean wave. Apparently someone—most likely Lady Durham—had passed the word that their rector had married. As men tend to do, Joseph seemed oblivious to the whispers and glances cast at her. But she wasn't.

Slowly, those who had been standing at the back of the room took their seats and after one more rap of the gavel, the room grew silent.

"Before we begin our meeting, I would like to take this opportunity to present my wife, Lady Abigail Fox." He held up his hand as questions rose from the crowd. "I will be happy to have you greet Lady Abigail when we are finished. I am sure you will all welcome her and make her feel at home here at St. Gertrude's."

Abigail's gaze roamed the room while Joseph spoke to his parishioners about the new school, and how beneficial it would be to their children. The women seemed much more interested in the rector's wife than the school. Most smiled shyly at her, a few of the younger ones with a bit of regret. Joseph had apparently been on several women's list of potential husbands.

Most of the members of Joseph's parish were hard working farmers and tradespeople. Before she and Joseph had taken their places at the head of the room, she'd been introduced to Baron Moreledge and his wife. The baron was very friendly, but the baroness took it upon herself to inform Abigail that there weren't too many people in Abbysby End who were of *their station*.

Abigail had chuckled to herself since it apparently hadn't occurred to the baroness that Joseph was not of *their station,* either. But aside from that remark, she seemed friendly enough, and offered to have Abigail to tea one afternoon so she could spend time with other women of the parish.

After Joseph's talk, a few of the parishioners had questions, mostly about how many hours a day the children would need to be away from home. It also appeared the tradespeople and shopkeepers saw more of a benefit to the school than the farmers did. No surprise there.

"That is all I have to say about the school right now. If there are no further questions, then we can enjoy the punch and biscuits the ladies have prepared for us." Joseph turned to Abigail. "Perhaps it would be best if you joined the other ladies for refreshments."

She nodded and headed to the table where the women

had gathered.

"Mrs. Fox," one of the women greeted her, "so nice of you to join us."

"Wilma, it is not Mrs. Fox, but Lady Abigail. Didn't you listen when Mr. Fox introduced her?" A rotund woman did a slight curtsey to Abigail as she cast a disparaging glance at the hapless matron.

"That is quite all right. And who may you be?" Abigail asked the first woman.

"My lady, I am Mrs. Richard Steeves. My husband is a solicitor. I'm sorry to greet you incorrectly." She blushed and wrung her hands.

"Please, do not distress yourself." Abigail turned an inquisitive eye to the other woman.

"My lady, I am Widow Barnes. I do sewing for the village. Mr. Fox has graciously allowed me to do some tailoring for him, but I am sure your ladyship has a wonderful *modiste* in London."

Abigail smiled warmly at the widow. "Indeed I do, but I doubt if I will have time to travel to London if I need any new frocks. I'm sure you will do nicely to accommodate me."

Widow Barnes swallowed several times, appearing to almost cry with pleasure. "That is most kind of you, my lady."

"Lady Abigail, so nice to see you again." Lady Durham stepped to Abigail's side and embraced her as if they were long-lost friends.

A bit surprised at the warm welcome, she murmured, "And you too, Lady Durham."

Lady Durham faced the women in their circle. "I was honored to be introduced to Lady Abigail this morning." She beamed at Abigail, seeming to have recovered from the shock she'd received at their breakfast table. "I am sure she will be a wonderful addition to our little group."

"Lady Abigail, you must join us for tea one day next week," Mrs. Steeves said. "We take turns hosting our gathering of ladies. We sew baby clothes for the poor."

"Indeed," Lady Durham said. "I will be happy to stop by to escort you in my carriage."

Several women came and went to their little group, all very pleasant and welcoming. It was nice to be so quickly accepted by Joseph's people. She'd been invited to several teas, and offers to have her and Joseph to dinner.

"My dear, I think it is time we departed." Joseph walked up behind her and squeezed her elbow. "Ladies, if you will excuse us."

"Certainly, Mr. Fox," Widow Barnes said. "I imagine you are both still fatigued from your trip from London."

"Yes, and Lady Abigail sustained an injury the day we arrived, and she should not be overtiring herself."

"Oh, my lady, I hope you are all right." Lady Durham was the epitome of solicitude.

"I am fine. It was a minor mishap." She turned to Joseph. "I *am* tired, perhaps it is best if we take our leave."

After a quick good-bye they withdrew, leaving Abigail with a warm feeling from the women she'd met. Life here could be very pleasant.

• • •

"Would you care for a sherry before bed?" Joseph asked from the sideboard where he splashed some brandy into his glass.

"Yes. Perhaps I will."

He poured the drink and after handing it to Abigail, settled in the chair across from her.

"I received the final sketches from the contractor. They had apparently been delivered while we were at the meeting this evening."

"Wonderful. I am anxious to see them. Did he include the suggested changes I made so there is a quiet space for the children to read? I envision some type of a small library."

"Yes. I am very pleased with the results. And I must thank you once again for your very insightful ideas."

A comfortable silence followed as they both sipped their drinks.

"Mrs. O'Neill was kind enough to give me a tour of the house today."

"Ah. I hope you found everything to your liking?"

"Yes." Her slight hesitation and then charming flush left him thinking she wanted to discuss something different. A more important topic. Hopefully she was ready to be his wife in truth, since he'd been thinking of nothing else all day.

Whatever was supposed to be occupying his thoughts had not been enough to keep his mind from drifting toward Abigail and her luscious body. He'd been embarrassed when several times the contractor had to repeat himself to get a proper answer.

The next appointment for the day had been a young couple casting each other shy and loving glances. The interview to arrange for their banns to be announced only reinforced his decision to stop this game Abigail was playing. He didn't know how much longer he was willing to put up with it nor did he understand where her reluctance came from.

The meeting tonight had not engaged his attention fully, either. He'd watched her as she spoke with the ladies of the parish, all the time planning how he could get her away from the group and headed home. To bed.

The word *bed* caught his attention.

"During my time with Mrs. O'Neill today, it came to my attention that the bedchamber you brought me to yesterday was yours."

He nodded.

Finally, a conversation I can concentrate on.

"Right. Well, I guess what I want to know is. . ." She stopped, licked her lips and started again. "I mean, is it your intention. . ."

"Out with it, Abigail. Or should I save you this unnecessary embarrassment, and tell you that yes, I do intend for my wife to sleep in my bed?"

She sniffed. "Yes. That is precisely what I wanted to know."

"Now you have your answer." He raised his hand as she opened her mouth to speak. "Please don't tell me about separate sleeping quarters being *de rigueur* for the *ton*. I am aware that your parents shared a bed—no need for you to know how I came about that information—as does your brother and his wife. Therefore, this is not a foreign concept."

Her eyes narrowed. "Just for your information, I was not about to dispute that, or mention what is done among the members of the *ton*." Then a small smile teased her lips. "How *do* you know the sleeping arrangements for my family members?"

"You forget that I practically lived at your house in my

youth. It was well known that your parents did not sleep apart."

"And Drake?"

He grinned. "That was a guess."

"A good one, however."

Joseph placed his glass next to him and leaned forward, his forearms resting on his knees. "I always expected to marry. When I first finished theology school, I was busy with my parish, getting to know the villagers and helping out where I could. The rector before me was aged, and apparently did very little in the way of ministering to his people.

"They were starved for comfort and spirituality. I like to think I helped in that way." He sat back and crossed his arms over his chest. "But I've known for a while now that the time was right for me to take a wife. You must understand, Abigail that I never would have looked toward you, or anyone in your station."

"Joseph—"

"Let me finish, please." He waited for a moment, gathering his thoughts. "When I say I would not have looked at you, I mean that despite our life-long friendship, I doubted your brother would have approved of me. Well, certainly as a friend, but not as a suitor for one of his sisters." He winced and ran his fingers through his hair. "I have a feeling I'm making a muddle of this."

"No, you're not. I understand what you're trying to say. However, you must realize that despite my ruined reputation, I still would not have consented to this marriage unless I felt we would do well together. And I am looking forward to being a rector's wife."

"A rector's wife or my wife? And in all ways?" His body

hummed with longing. Sitting there, her back stiff, with her hands crossed delicately in her lap, should not have made his blood boil, but boil it did.

She placed her glass on the table alongside her and eased herself from the chair. "I think I would like to retire now."

Before she was able to move two steps, he reached out and grabbed her hand, tugging her forward until she landed on his lap. "Not yet." He encircled her waist, trapping her. "There are matters we need to discuss."

"Yes." She cleared her throat. "In that case, I wanted to talk about my role in the school."

He pulled her closer and nuzzled her neck, the essence of flowers, and her own unique scent, heating his blood. "*I* want to talk about your role as my wife."

"Yes, that too…" Her voice drifted off as he placed tiny kisses along her jawline. She moved her head, giving him better access to the silky skin of her neck. God, how he wanted her. She shifted slightly on his lap, eliciting a groan from deep within his chest. He spread his fingers on her back, moving her closer, his other hand sliding up from her waist until it covered her breast.

Joseph kneaded the soft mound, squeezing, shaping. His thumb flicked over her nipple, satisfaction rushing through him when it pebbled, and she released a breathy sigh. Her quickened breath and flushed face told him his ministrations were working.

He moved his hand to cup the back of her head, easing her lips to his. His mouth demanded a response, and she gave it to him, parting her lips when he slid his tongue along their plumpness. Lips that were made for kissing. Which he did, while also nibbling, sucking, and licking until she made small mewling sounds.

His body caught fire as he swept into her mouth, touching all the sensitive parts, tasting her nectar. Unaware of what she was doing to him, she continued to shift in his lap, her restlessness causing him to go from readiness to pure agony.

. . .

Abigail eased her hands up Joseph's chest until she grasped his shoulders. Several times over the years she'd received a quick kiss in a darkened garden. Once she'd even been the recipient of a more-than-simple buss from one of London's most notorious rakes before her brother had discovered them and blackened the man's eye. But nothing had prepared her for her body's response to Joseph's kiss.

Every reasonable thought fled, and if she needed to put two words together to form a coherent sentence to save her life, she'd be dead. And the feelings!

A few more minutes, and her clothes would go up in flames. Joseph's hand on her breast, at first surprising, soon had her itching to remove her gown without appearing wanton. Her body ached to have his skin touching hers. The problem was solved when her bodice dropped to her waist. While she'd been a bit distracted, he'd unbuttoned her gown, and was now pushing down her chemise, exposing her to his hungry eyes.

The cool evening air puckered her nipples. Joseph drew back, his fingers gliding oh-so-softly over her breasts. She closed her eyes against the need in his eyes–a frightening thing.

"Abigail, you are so beautiful. I always thought… but never realized." His whispered words glided over her, making her feel beautiful, indeed. His hands covered her ribs, then slowly moved up, caressing both breasts. She arched her back, wanting more, desperately needing something else that she could not identify.

Unsatisfied at not being an active participant, she slid her fingers into his jacket and shoved it off his shoulders. Then she undid his cravat and quickly unbuttoned his lawn shirt, pushing the placket apart, smoothing her hands over the crisp hairs on his chest.

"Sweetheart, we should go upstairs," he mumbled right before he took her breast in his mouth, and she nearly slid to the floor. He teased her nipple with his tongue, and then suckled hard, a jolt of pleasure shooting from his mouth to her woman's core.

He drew back and pulled her bodice up, not bothering to fasten the buttons.

"What…what are you doing?" Was that her voice? It was thick, raspy. And why in heaven's name had he stopped doing whatever it was he was doing that felt so wonderful?

Instead of answering, he scooped her into his arms, and tucking her against his chest, headed for the door. She wrapped her arms around his neck, holding tightly as he took the stairs two at a time. He shifted her body so he was able to unlatch the bedchamber door. The distance between the door and the huge bed sitting in the middle of the room disappeared in a flash.

Joseph slid her down his body, easing off her clothing with nimble fingers, until she stood nude before him. Unwilling to be the only undressed member of the party, Abigail yanked at his jacket. He shrugged it off before pulling apart his shirt, buttons popping and flying in all directions.

Heat radiated from his body in waves. She ran her palms over his skin, fascinated as his muscles rippled under her touch. The crinkly hairs in the center of his chest ended at the top of his breeches, leaving her curious as to what followed.

His hands gripped her bottom, kneading, massaging, pulling her forward, against *it*. She moved her lower body, the friction sending jolts of pleasure from her woman's place right to her breasts. She moaned softly as he nuzzled her neck, whispering meaningless words in her ear. But the vibration of his chest against her body excited her, causing her breasts to swell, the nipples to bead.

All of her senses came alive. The scent of leather and Joseph, the taste of his skin, salty and spicy, as her lips, then the tip of her tongue, savored him. Within seconds he eased her back onto the bed, coming down to lie alongside her. He stroked his palm over her curves, from her breast to the dip at her waist to the rise of her hips. "Take out your pins," he whispered. His deep brown eyes had darkened to nearly black, the passion evident even in her innocence.

Abigail reached behind her and removed the hairpins. She shook her head, sending the length of her hair tumbling down her back. Joseph grasped the back of her neck and pulled her forward. Reclaiming her lips, he crushed her to him while his fingers laced through her hair, tangling in the mass.

He drew back and pulled her curls forward, so the strands rested on her breasts. "Your hair is like a curtain of velvet."

She closed her eyes. Her hair resting against her bare shoulders as he teased her nipple with the locks, heightened the dampness and throbbing in her lower parts.

She was on the verge of something momentous, a slow buildup of previously unknown pleasure. Rolling on top of her, his weight crushed her into the mattress. The contrast between the hardness of his body and her softness overwhelmed her senses. She traced her fingertips lightly over his arms, then encircled his neck, tugging him forward for a kiss. His tongue swept into her mouth, and she met his invasion with her own. As she dueled with him, a sense of urgency drove her, readying her for the next step.

Her body on fire, she ached for a way to release the tortuous need his assiduity had awoken in her. Surely there must be something he could do to relieve her of this torment. Almost as if he'd read her mind, Joseph eased away, a slow smile spreading across his face. "Don't go anywhere." Shocked at the coolness that wafted over her skin at the loss of his heat, she rose up on her elbows as he removed his stockings and boots. He unfastened his breeches, and her breath hitched. He shoved his breeches down, his gaze never leaving hers. Her eyes grew wide and she backed up until she was at the very edge of the bed.

She shook her head. "No."

"It's all right, sweetheart." He climbed in next to her, and wrapped his arm around her waist, pulling her forward.

"No."

"There is nothing to worry about."

"No."

• • •

No amount of words was going to ease her mind, so Joseph pulled Abigail to his body and cupped her face. He started at her forehead, and leaving a trail of kisses, worked his way down to her nose, cheeks, chin, chest, and then took her breast into his mouth and suckled. He smiled at the sigh of pleasure that came from her lips, at the way her tense muscles eased.

Once she seemed more relaxed, he moved his hand down to her feminine heat, surprised and pleased to find her swollen and wet. His fingers moved over her, stroking and caressing.

"Oh, my." She shifted beneath him, pressing her nether parts against his fingers.

"Like that, do you?" he asked.

"Yes." The word came out on a whispery gasp.

He studied her as he continued his ministrations. Her eyes were closed, a slight smile on her face. The flush on her cheeks and the increase in her breathing told him how close she was to her release. He thought of all the things he could do to bring her to completion, but he would save those. As an innocent, he didn't want to scandalize her the first time. But as he licked her nipples, the restless movement of her legs played havoc with his control.

He shifted until he was over her, his fingers still busy. A soft keening sound started in her chest, and she stiffened and pressed her legs together, pushing so hard on his hand that she lifted them both off the bed. "Joseph," she cried out.

"I'm here, my sweet."

Once she slumped, he spread her legs further apart with his knees and slowly began to enter her. She opened her eyes, a siren's smile on her lips as she brushed back the hair falling over his brow. He lowered his head and moved his mouth over hers, devouring its softness. His forehead beaded with sweat as he took her inch by inch, enveloped by her warmth and moistness.

"It feels so odd."

"Am I hurting you?" His jaw tightened as he attempted to hold himself back.

She shook her head.

He continued until he met her resistance. Braced on his elbows, he held her face and whispered, "I'm sorry." He thrust forward, but no cry erupted from her mouth. Instead, a small tear leaked from her eye that he brushed away with his thumb. "Are you all right?"

She nodded, and after a minute, shifted under him. Encouraged by her movement, he began the rhythm that would bring him a much needed release. He lowered his head to her neck where he whispered words of her beauty, of the feel of her soft, plush body, what she was doing to him, how much he desired her. Abigail wrapped her legs around his hips, tilting herself as he went deeper. She clutched his arms, her nails digging deep, rolling her head back and forth.

It had been some time since he'd lain with a woman, so within minutes he felt close to an explosion. Throwing his head back, he groaned as he shuddered with release. Without conscious thought, he collapsed on top of her, his breathing so erratic he felt as though all the air in the world had vanished.

Chapter Seven

Abigail frowned at the burst of sunlight in her face. Still half asleep, she eased her eyes open to see Joseph standing by the window, apparently having just secured the cord on the drapes.

He was naked. Oh, dear. All golden skin and muscular body. Muscles that rippled as he drew back the other drape and secured the cord.

Memories of the several times they'd made love the previous night swept over her, coinciding with the wave of heat that started at her toes and went directly to her face.

"Good morning, sweetheart."

Now why did that endearment bother her so much? Lord knew the man had used it enough last night when they were...

But now in the morning light, it seemed a bit too intimate. She didn't want to be his sweetheart, only his partner. In fact, she wasn't at all happy with the look on his face. His demeanor held an expectation of something beyond the possible procreation of a child; perhaps a shift in their relationship.

She needed to disavow him of any ideas along that line. He'd agreed to sharing the marriage bed until she was increasing. As soon as she had proof of that condition, she would move into the other bedroom.

Suddenly aware that she, too, was without clothing, she tugged the covers up to her neck. "Good morning." Lifting her chin, she assessed him coolly. "If you will be so kind as to ring for my lady's maid, I would like a bath this morning." She stared at him directly. "In my bedchamber."

At her words, his smile dimmed and his expression changed to one of aloofness, but not before she saw the light of *something* leave his eyes. She pushed away the prickling of guilt. Surely he wasn't developing a *tendre* for her? She must put an end to that immediately.

He nodded. "As you wish." He strode to the door, grabbing his banyan on the way and shrugging into it. He alerted a footman to send Sanders to her ladyship's bedchamber.

Not sure how to exit gracefully, her gown nowhere to be seen, Abigail wrapped herself in the sheet and made a quick escape through the door adjoining the two chambers.

She breathed a sigh of relief and leaned against the closed door. She'd hurt Joseph, but it couldn't be helped. He had agreed to her conditions, after all. Better for him to have a small hurt now, than for her to have to grapple with a large hurt later. Love was fleeting, she'd discovered.

No, it was better this way. Let her and Joseph stay friends and partners. They would build a life of contentment and productivity. They would create a fine school and make a difference in the lives of his parishioners. That was her goal. And if things were to remain pleasant between them, it had better be his goal as well.

"Here we are, my lady." Sanders, her lady's maid, entered the room in front of a footman carrying a large bathtub. He set it alongside the fireplace. Two maids followed with buckets of water, as the footman started a fire in the hearth.

She'd been surprised to discover during the tour with Mrs. O'Neill yesterday that in addition to the housekeeper, Joseph employed Manning—his butler who doubled as a valet when needed—a cook, two maids, two footmen, a gardener, and a stable man. A miniscule staff compared to what she was used to, but nevertheless, more servants than she'd expected. She was especially pleased with Sanders, who was Cook's niece. So far she'd proven to be quite a proficient lady's maid.

Joseph had even indicated that if she felt it necessary to add to the household, she merely needed to tell Mrs. O'Neill to secure more help. Yes, life here could be quite pleasant. If she could keep her distance from her husband.

Once the tub was filled and the servants gone, she sank gratefully into its warmth. The slight soreness between her legs eased as the hot water surrounded her. Admittedly, the discomfort she'd experienced paled compared to the pleasure that had brought the minor pain about.

Truth be known, she'd thoroughly enjoyed Joseph's attentions last evening. Leaning her head back, she closed her eyes and relived their time together, amazed that every joining had been as good as the first.

The night before, after their breathing had returned to

normal for the last time, Joseph had wrapped his arm around her waist and pulled her to him, her back to his chest. She'd relished the warmth, but somehow the position seemed more intimate than what they'd just done.

Then as she drifted off to sleep, she felt him nuzzling her neck, and whispering in her ear. She tried to remember the words he'd murmured, but to no avail.

"My lady, shall I wash your hair now?" Sanders bustled into the room, several drying cloths draped over her arm. "Then I'll brush out the tangles while you sit by the fire."

Wrenched from her meanderings, Abigail sat forward so the maid could minister to her, all thoughts of Joseph and his lovemaking relegated to a place in her mind called *visit-with-care*.

· · ·

Joseph entered the breakfast room to find it empty. Not that he'd expected Abigail to arrive before him. He assumed ladies and their baths took quite some time.

The enticing aroma of eggs, kippers, ham slices, and herring in cream sauce, laid out on the table, along with toast, fresh rolls, and coffee reminded him how hungry he was. Perhaps all the activity last evening had increased his appetite. At least one appetite had been appeased. For now.

Once his plate was filled, he took his place at the head of the table, glancing at the setting to his right where his wife would join him.

His wife.

Fool he, to think last night had changed anything between them. Abigail had been just as aloof this morning as she'd been the day she'd accepted his *proposal* and laid out the rules of how they would go on. No doubt she would have felt quite differently had Redgrave been in her bed.

His stomach tightened at the thought of the cad. Were he ever to meet up with the man, he would find a great deal of satisfaction in plowing his fist into Redgrave's nose. Then he would shake his hand in thanks for making it possible for him to have Abigail as his wife.

If she only desired his friendship and his seed, he would work to change her mind. She wanted to be mistress of her own home and have children. He had required money. Although such arrangements were so basic, and typical of the upper crust, he had no plans of being satisfied with those terms, despite Abigail's intentions.

"I believe the lovely scent of breakfast led me directly here." Abigail entered, her usual sunny disposition back in place. She smiled at him as he held out her chair, then looked away. "I am quite ravenous this morning."

Joseph refrained from pointing out his previous observation that their night time activities might have spurred their hunger. "I will send for tea. My footman is used to having coffee for me at breakfast."

"Yes, thank you. That would be lovely."

"Or do you prefer chocolate?"

"No, thank you. Tea will be fine."

He signaled to the footman, who hurried away to do as he bid. "May I fill a plate for you?"

"No. Thank you, I prefer to make a selection." She eyed the offerings. "Everything looks wonderful."

Joseph's appetite vanished, and not because he'd eaten part of his meal. The conversation between himself and his wife was so stilted and awkward, it was almost as if they'd just met in a London ballroom. Dear God, they were husband and wife, had known each other all their lives, and had shared a bed last night.

"Abigail."

"Yes?"

"Look at me."

Apparently attuned to his mood, she placed her hands in her lap and studied him.

Joseph leaned back and crossed his arms. "What is the matter?"

"I have no idea what you mean."

"Yes, you do. You're an intelligent woman—" he paused as the footman entered and placed the teapot in front of them.

"Thank you," she said. "What was your name again? I'm afraid I've forgotten."

"Posey, my lady."

"I shall remember the next time."

"That's all, Posey. You may leave us now." Joseph waited until the footman quietly closed the door, then he turned to Abigail. "About last night."

"Yes. It was a lovely meeting, and I enjoyed spending time with the ladies. I think it will be beneficial for me to join their group. They are sewing baby clothes for the poor. It seems like a very worthwhile project…"

He allowed her to go on about the meeting as she obviously did not want to discuss the same activities of last night that he wished to discuss. Two red spots appeared on her cheeks as she jerkily poured tea for herself, her words tripping over each other. Feeling a bit of sympathy for her unease, he merely smiled as her comments faltered and then stopped.

"I am glad you enjoyed meeting my parishioners. And I believe joining the women's sewing circle is an excellent idea." He checked his pocket watch. "However, I fear I must leave you now. I am expecting a visit from a young man I've been tutoring in preparation for his entry into University."

"Oh." The air seemed to leave her, like a deflated ball. "Perhaps I will take a stroll after breakfast. I should like to walk to the village and meet those who were not in attendance last evening."

On his way out, Joseph brushed a kiss over her forehead. "That sounds like a wonderful idea. I shall be tied up for the morning, so perhaps I will join you for luncheon?"

Abigail nodded, unaware that he watched her from the doorway as she touched her fingertips to the spot he had kissed. His stomach knotted in frustration, he continued down the corridor.

• • •

The scent of newly awakened flowers filled the late spring air. The half hour walk to the village gave Abigail plenty of time to muse over her new life. It had seemed strange this morning to not spend time going through invitations, admiring bouquets of flowers from potential suitors, and receiving callers—her life as it had been since she'd left the schoolroom. Now she was a married woman with responsibilities beyond her expected realm.

As she entered the village proper, the lure of meat pies drew her into the first shop. The flush-faced woman behind the counter was selling her wares as quickly as she took them out of the oven. Abigail joined the queue, introducing herself to those she hadn't yet met. Most people had already heard of Joseph's marriage, and welcomed her warmly.

With a smile on her face and a warm meat pie in her hand, she left the shop and continued on her way. Being a market town, Addysby End boasted a number of shops, as well as a small circulating library and an inn.

"Lady Abigail!"

She turned to see a young woman with a babe in her arms hurrying toward her. Taking a moment to catch her breath, she startled Abigail by bursting into tears. "Oh, dear. I'm nothing more than a watering pot."

Abigail touched the woman lightly on her arm. "It is all right. Is there something I can help you with?"

The woman wiped the tears from her face and shook her head. "No. You have done so much for me already."

When Abigail regarded her with raised eyebrows, she continued. "You rescued my little girl from being attacked by our pig a few days ago."

"You must be Agnes's mother. Mrs. Dinger, correct?"

"Yes, I am. I meant to attend the meeting last night about the school so I could thank you then, but this one,"—she nodded toward the baby settled firmly on her hip—"decided to raise a fuss about going to sleep, and Mr. Dinger is not too handy with the children."

"It was no trouble for me. Is Agnes recovered from her fright?"

"Oh, she is fine, but I see you still have scratches on your face. I am so sorry that nasty pig got out to begin with. I've told my boys to be careful with latching the fence."

"I am happy your little girl wasn't injured."

Mrs. Dinger smiled, a slight blush on her cheeks. "Well, thank you again. If there is ever anything I can do for you…"

"I will be sure to ask. It was a pleasure meeting you." Abigail touched the baby's sweet cheek with the back of her hand and continued on her way. Perhaps one day she would have a little one of her own in her arms. She thought of a boy with Joseph's deep brown eyes and wavy black hair. An imp with a smile that would wrap her around his tiny finger. Or a little girl with curly black hair, who would surely wrap her father around her finger.

For the first time, she realized her children would not be *Lady* or *Lord*. Not that titles mattered so much to her, as it wasn't something she'd ever thought about one way or another, since she'd just assumed it would be so. At least with her and Joseph's connections, and their sufficient funds, any children of theirs would certainly be able to take their place among Polite Society when the time came. She would have to be careful with their education and make sure they had all the advantages they would have enjoyed had she'd married Redgrave.

Redgrave. Just the thought of him brought shivers to her. What a bounder the man had turned out to be. Despite the disgrace his abandonment had caused her, she was grateful that his wicked side had emerged before they had irrevocably joined themselves together. Now if she could only erase him from her heart, all would be well.

She wiped her fingers on the handkerchief in her reticule and glanced down the street. The small circulating library caught her eye, and she headed straight for it. The town certainly boasted enough shops to keep her well supplied.

In fact, she need never return to London if she wished. At one time that thought would have panicked her. Now it was comforting. Village life was very appealing.

The tinkle of a bell sounded as she opened the door of the circulating library. The welcoming and familiar scent of paper and leather drifted toward her. Shelves of books lined the walls, and an older man sat at a desk near the door, writing in some type of a ledger. He looked up as she entered and smiled. "You must be the rector's new wife. Lady Abigail."

"Yes, I am."

"I am Mr. Fogel. We were all happy to hear Mr. Fox had married. Although I'm sure some of the ladies who had their eye on him weren't too pleased." His warm smile and twinkling eyes brought a grin to her face.

"I would like to take a look at your books."

"Go right ahead, my lady. If I can help in any way, please let me know."

A few hours later, Abigail peeked at the position of the sun outside the little shop's window, amazed at how quickly the time had passed. A few people had come and gone, and Mr. Fogel was careful to introduce her to everyone who came in. She enjoyed meeting the townsfolk.

She stretched to loosen her tight muscles and picked up two books from the stack alongside her that seemed interesting. Since she'd already missed luncheon with her husband, if she were to meet him for tea, she must hurry.

After paying her two guineas for a year's subscription, she waved goodbye to Mr. Fogel and left the library. The streets were not as busy as when she'd arrived earlier. Fewer shoppers strolled along, although the woman who'd sold her the meat pie seemed to still be doing a brisk business. Her stomach growling, Abigail waved at her and crossed the street in the direction of home.

. . .

Joseph checked his pocket watch one more time. Tea had come and gone, and Abigail had still not returned. He never should have allowed her to walk to the village by herself. Even though it was a straight path, she could have gotten turned around, and now be wandering in circles.

He rose from his desk and strolled to the window, telling himself he wasn't concerned, but merely wanted to see how the gardener's work was progressing.

No sign of her coming up the road.

One more turn around the room and he strode to the front door and headed to the stable. "Jackson, please tack up Whitney."

"Yes, sir." The stable master laid aside the bridle he'd been working on. While Joseph paced, Jackson readied his horse. His carriage might have been a better idea to retrieve her, but the horse would be faster. The tiny kernel of fear in his belly had grown as the sun began its descent behind the trees.

He jumped on Whitney the minute Jackson brought him out. Since the village wasn't too far, he hoped the daylight would last long enough to do a thorough search.

Keeping the horse at a trot, he scanned the area, his fear mounting as he grew closer to town with no sign of Abigail. This had to be the path she would have taken, going directly from his house to the main part of town.

About a mile before the stone wall surrounding the town appeared, he spotted a lump on the ground ahead of him, off to the side. Anyone passing by would not have seen it, only if they looked directly at that spot. He squeezed his thighs to kick Whitney into a gallop, leading him over brambles until he reached what looked like a bundle of rags on the ground.

He slid off the horse and dropped to his knees. "Abigail!" She lay on her stomach, her face in a cluster of leaves. As he rolled her over, he noticed a gash on her forehead. He felt for her pulse, releasing the breath he held. Faint, but steady.

The air had chilled, and her clothes were damp from lying on the ground. He needed to get her home and into bed. Scooping her into his arms, he held her close to his chest as he put his foot into the stirrup, then swung his leg over Whitney. Settling her on his lap as best he could, he took off toward home.

"Send for the surgeon," Joseph barked as he once again strode past a surprised Manning with his wife in his arms. "And ask Mrs. O'Neill to come to my bedchamber at once."

Joseph hurried up the steps, shifting Abigail in order to open the door. Once inside, he laid her gently on the bed and studied her face.

"Sir, Manning said you wished to see me." Mrs. O'Neill stopped at the foot of the bed, her fingers pressed against her mouth. "Oh, dear, what has happened to my lady?"

"I'm not quite sure. I found her about a mile from the village. She has a gash on her forehead, which I believe might have come from her falling against a rock. I've sent for the surgeon."

"What can I do, sir?"

"Please light candles. Plenty of them. Then ask Sanders

to attend my wife. She'll need to remove these damp clothes."
He turned as Mrs. O'Neill headed to the door. "Also ask one
of the footmen to light a fire. I need it warm in here so her
ladyship doesn't catch a chill."

"Yes, sir."

Joseph sat alongside her on the bed and took her cold
hand in his. "Abigail, what in heaven's name did you do?"
Even though he knew she couldn't hear him, it made him
feel better to talk to her, pretend she could hear him, assume
she would be all right.

"Oh, my poor lady. What is wrong?" Her eyes wide,
Sanders approached the bed.

"She apparently fell and struck her head. Please remove
her clothes and get her into a warm nightgown." He turned
toward the door. "Where is the blasted footman?"

"Right here, sir," David, the younger footman said, as
he hurried through the doorway carrying a bucket of coal.
With efficient movements, he went about starting a fire. In
the meantime, Mrs. O'Neill lit a number of candles about
the room.

In the candlelight Abigail looked like she was sleeping.
He ran his fingers over the scratches from her encounter
with the Dinger's pig. Now she had a gash on her forehead
from heaven knew what. He was certainly not doing a very
good job of protecting his wife.

"I will await the surgeon downstairs."

After telling Manning to alert him the minute the
surgeon arrived, he cosseted himself in his study. With shaky
hands he poured a brandy and wandered to the library
window. Nothing but the darkness of night greeted him.

He hadn't spent a great deal of time studying the area

where he'd found Abigail, but couldn't for the life of him imagine how she'd ended up on the ground with a gash on her forehead. Had she tripped? Twisted her ankle on a rabbit hole? He shook his head, then took another sip of brandy. Once she awoke—and he prayed that would be soon—he would get to the bottom of this.

"Sir?"

Joseph turned as Sanders pushed open the door, Abigail's frock over her arm. "Yes?"

"I don't mean to intrude, Mr. Fox, but Mrs. O'Neill thought perhaps we should show this to you."

"You did not leave her ladyship alone, I hope?"

She shook her head furiously. "No, sir. Mrs. O'Neill is with her."

He breathed a sigh of relief. "What is it you wish to show me?"

She moved forward and held the dress out to him. "Mrs. O'Neill and I discovered this when we undressed her ladyship."

He looked at her with raised eyebrows. "You wished to show me her gown?"

"No, sir. I wanted to show you the bullet hole we found in the sleeve."

Chapter Eight

Joseph felt all the blood leave his face and pool at his feet. "Bullet?" he croaked.

"Yes, sir." Sanders moved closer and stuck her finger through the hole in the sleeve of Abigail's silk gown. She wiggled her finger back and forth until Joseph thought he would cast up his accounts.

"Enough!"

"Oh, sorry, sir." She backed away, her eyes downcast.

Guilt nudged him for taking out his anger and frustration on the poor maid. What was that quote about being the bearer of bad news? After apologizing and dismissing her, he rested his hands on his hips, studying the carpet, his thoughts in a whirl. Turning on his heel, he strode to the window, trying hard to get himself under control.

A bullet? Why would someone shoot Abigail? It must have been a hunter not being careful enough. Bloody hell, this marriage might have saved his wife from scandal, but it was becoming very dangerous to her well-being. She'd been here only three days and injured twice.

"Sir, the surgeon has arrived." Manning stuck his head around the partially closed door.

"Thank you, Manning." Joseph grabbed the frock from the chair where Sanders had dropped it, and left the room.

Mrs. O'Neill had done a good job of placing enough candles and two oil lamps around the room. Abigail lay still on the bed, the surgeon on a chair next to her, examining her arm closely. "Mr. Fox, it appears your wife not only hit her head when she fell, but she also sustained a bullet wound to her right arm." He looked up at Joseph as he strode into the room, the garment still clutched in his fist.

"I have just been informed of that fact. How serious?"

"Only a flesh wound. I found very little in the way of fabric imbedded into the wound. Her maid tells me she wore a silk gown, which is fortunate for her. Silk lessens the depth of the piercing, so there were no nasty pieces of wool to pull from her injury. My main concern is the loss of blood, and the damage to her head." He returned his attention to his work, then spoke over his shoulder. "How did her ladyship end up with a bullet wound?"

"That is something I intend to find out. She had planned a walk to the village. I worried about her going alone, but it never occurred to me that something like this would happen. You can be assured she will not venture beyond the front door by herself ever again."

Joseph moved closer to the bed, and took the cloth Mrs. O'Neill had been using to wipe Abigail's brow. "I will tend to her now. Please prepare one of your elixirs for her ladyship. I am concerned about infection and would like to have something to offer her when she awakens." The doctor turned to the housekeeper. "Madam, if the household also stores honey, please bring some. It will help to cut down on the infection and reduce the size and appearance of any resulting scar by keeping the skin around the wound moist and soft."

"Honey?" Joseph asked as Mrs. O'Neill hurried from the room.

"Yes. I spent some years in the Far East during my youth and learned they used honey for dressing wounds. Although no one is quite sure why it helps, it does appear to be very beneficial."

Sometime later, Joseph jerked awake as his head fell forward. Confused for the moment, he eased his sore muscles from the cramped position he'd been in on the chair next to Abigail's bed. He ran his palm down his face and shook the sleep from his body. He'd been sitting in the chair for hours.

The faint light of dawn brought Abigail's features into view, a soft glow from the window casting her skin in a milky white luster. Her dark eyelashes rested on her pale cheeks like chocolate crescents.

While he studied her, she slowly opened her eyes, blinking as if unsure where she was. "Joseph?"

He leaned forward and took her hand in his. "How do you feel, sweetheart?"

"Like I was stomped by a horse. What happened to me?"

Brushing back the errant curls from her forehead, he said, "You had an accident coming back from town. Do you remember anything?"

She licked her lips and furrowed her brows. "I'm not sure. I think I remember walking home, and then, something happened." She stopped and shook her head slightly, then winced. "Goodness, my head hurts like the devil."

"You must have fallen and hit your head on a protrusion, most likely a rock."

"Fell? That explains it. Have I been unconscious?"

"For about ten hours."

She closed her eyes, leaving him to wonder if he'd lost her again.

"May I have a drink of water?" she asked him through cracked lips.

"Of course." He reached behind him and retrieved a glass from the dresser.

She reached for the glass. "Ouch!" She sucked in a breath, growing pale. Her head dropped back onto the pillow. "If I fell and hit my head, why does my arm hurt so much?"

He placed the glass on the small table next to her bed and took her hand, not saying anything for a moment. He eyed her as he kissed her knuckles, then ran them over his lips.

"Joseph?"

When he didn't answer, she said, "What happened to my arm?"

"You were shot."

"Shot!" Her jaw dropped and her eyes widened. "I was shot?"

He nodded. The guilt at having brought her to a place where she'd had to rescue a child from a charging pig, then suffered a bullet wound, sickened him. Dear God, what she must think of him and his village? The rage that rose up when he'd first heard about the shooting threatened to engulf him again, twisting his gut, causing his hand to itch, wanting to punch his fist into something. Or some*one*.

"I spoke to the constabulary and the decision was that a careless hunter let go a poorly aimed shot." He held the glass of water to her lips. "Easy. Don't take too much."

The constabulary's announcement did not sit well. The road he'd found Abigail on was not a place where hunters would be found. It was a well-trafficked path used by villagers going to and from town. In fact, the place where he'd found her might not even have been where she had been shot. Well off the beaten path, it was quite possible the shooter had dragged her farther from the road.

Abigail took a few sips and wincing with pain, eased back down again. "I'm quite cold. Can you see about building up the fire?"

Joseph leaned down to kiss her forehead, the method his mother used when he was a youth to determine if he had a fever. Her skin was dry and warm. No doubt infection had set in, rendering her chilled. "I'll send for more coal, but in the meantime, I'll bundle you up with blankets."

"Th-th-ank you."

After covering her with more bedding, he notified the footman to bring additional coal and asked that he have Mrs. O'Neill prepare more of the elixir for infection.

For the next couple of days, Abigail shivered and demanded more heat, then threw off the many blankets he'd tucked around her and attempted to remove her night gown.

Joseph vacillated from pacing the room in agitation to sitting by her side, just staring at her. He rarely left the room, snapping at Mrs. O'Neill when she suggested she take a turn with Abigail, and allow him to sleep or eat other than from a tray brought to the room twice a day by the footman.

Manning showed up each morning to shave and admonish him—by forceful looks—on his disarray. He didn't care. When he grew too fatigued to even keep his eyes open, he'd crawled onto the bed and lay alongside his wife, holding her close when she shivered, and wiping her with a cloth when she perspired.

How frightening to watch someone you cared about toss and turn, mumbling incoherent words. She begged for water, which he ended up spilling all over her nightgown as she thrashed about in her fever-induced frenzy. He'd soon given up having Sanders change her, and did the chore himself, wincing each time he saw the bullet wound. Evidence of his neglect. Keeping her quiet became difficult, and he worried that she would break open the stitches.

On the fourth morning, he stood alongside the bed, taking in her wax-like countenance as the sun rose slowly over the horizon and bathed the entire room with light. Never in his entire life had he felt so helpless. He'd attended many a sick bed in his time as rector. Always, he would leave the distraught patient's loved one with words of comfort. He now realized they meant absolutely nothing. No words of comfort would relieve the fear of losing Abigail.

Weary to his soul, he removed his boots and stockings and crawled in alongside his wife.

• • •

Abigail opened her eyes to a disheveled Joseph lying alongside her. It appeared he'd had scant grooming or a change of clothing for days. His cravat and jacket were gone, and several buttons down the front of his linen shirt had been unfastened. He wore breeches, but his feet were bare of stockings and boots.

She had memories of him forcing liquid down her throat and wiping her with a cloth when she would have preferred to run naked in the cold. Her body itched with dried perspiration, and she had a horrible feeling she actually smelled.

Lightly she ran her fingertip over his eyebrow. He jerked but didn't open his eyes. She grinned as his lips twitched in the shadow of a smile. No doubt he'd taken care of her the entire time she'd been sick. Many men would have depended on servants to minister to a patient. There must have been a great deal of work he'd put off to remain here with her.

Joseph was proving to be a good husband. Just viewing the lines of weariness in his face and the dark circles under his eyes indicated he would always take care of her. As she studied him, a slight fluttering in her belly reminded her that she didn't want to dwell too much on his goodness. Theirs was not a love match, and she intended to keep it that way. One could not suffer a broken heart if one's heart was not engaged.

She moved her arm, but the pain was not as bad as it had been the last time she'd awoken. She shifted her gaze to study the canopy above her, trying to remember what had happened. Once she'd left the circulating library, she'd hurried on her way, anxious to make it home in time for tea. She'd passed a few people whom she had recognized, but instead of stopping to chat, she'd wished them a good day and had continued on.

Once she'd passed the stone wall surrounding the town proper, she hadn't seen anyone else until she awoke in bed. She wracked her brain trying to visualize the scene. It seemed to her there had been a noise and then a sharp pain in her upper arm before she'd either swooned or tripped on something and fell. Her memory provided no more than that.

She sighed and looked out the window on the far side of the room. The sun was full in the sky, indicating the time grew close to luncheon. She suddenly realized how very hungry she was. At least her headache was gone, and the pain somewhat diminished. She attempted to sit up, but the soreness of her arm, and the dizziness in her head drew her right back down again.

"What are you doing?"

She started at the sound of Joseph's voice. She turned to look at him, his chocolate brown eyes peering at her from underneath his thick brows.

"I think I would like something to eat. Or perhaps a bath. Yes, a bath first, then something to eat."

Joseph propped himself up on his elbow and studied her. "How do you feel?"

"Sore. Dizzy. Hungry. Dirty." She tilted her head. "How long have I been sick?"

"This is the fourth day."

"And from the looks of you, I would say you've been here the entire time."

He sat up and swung his legs over the edge of the bed. "You were quite sick there for a while."

She touched his back. "Thank you for taking care of me."

"You are my wife. And it is my fault that you were injured."

So it was only duty that kept him by her side. She

should have known his compassion and caring would insist he tend to her himself. Certainly no warm feelings for her. She thought back to his last comment. "Your fault? I don't understand. How is it your fault that I was shot and then landed on a rock?"

"I never should have allowed you to walk to the village. Especially by yourself. I am so sorry for all that has happened to you since your arrival."

"It was not a matter of you *letting* me walk to the village. I chose to do that."

"No, sweetheart, it is my job to protect you. To keep you safe. I haven't done a very good job of it, I'm afraid."

"I'm sure it is as the constabulary said, and a hunter was careless, causing my injuries."

"Perhaps. But to be on the safe side, I would prefer you to take the carriage on your next foray into town. In fact, I insist upon going with you."

She raised her chin. "I do not need an escort."

"Nevertheless, you will inform me if you wish to make visits so I might accompany you."

Abigail's eyebrows rose. "I'm to be a prisoner?" She bristled at the idea that she needed his permission to go somewhere. Whenever her brother had taken that attitude with her, or her sisters, they had quickly put him in his place. Although, truth be told, none of them had ever been shot at.

"Of course not. I only want to keep you safe."

"Has anyone else in Addysby End fallen victim to a shooting while walking to town?"

He shook his head.

"There, you see? It was a careless hunter, and it shall never happen again."

His jaw tightened and his eyes flashed. "I agree. It will never happen again because in the future I will not permit you to hie off to the village by yourself."

Oh, how dare the man be so pompous? As if she would ask his permission to leave the house. He would soon understand that she did not take well to being told what to do. And furthermore, waiting around like some simpering miss to have him escort her hither and yon was completely out of the question. "And how do you intend to do that, *Mr. Fox*, by tying me to this bed?" She slapped her hand down on the mattress, wincing at the pain that reverberated through her body at the unwise move.

In a flash, he joined her on the bed, his hands planted firmly on either side of her hips, his face mere inches from hers. "Be warned, *Lady Abigail*, if I tie you to this bed it will be for purposes other than to keep you from going to the village on your own."

Well, then.

Even in her innocence, his comment conjured up pictures that had heat spreading from her toes all the way to her hairline. She'd once snuck a book from her brother's room that she and Marion had giggled over before he'd caught them and lectured them for over an hour. One picture in particular came to mind now. Her mouth formed a small circle.

The look in his eyes had turned from anger to something else in a flash. Goodness, but she felt warm of a sudden. She raised her hand to her forehead. Perhaps her fever had returned.

A tap on the door brought their attention to Sanders as she entered the room. "I heard my lady's voice, sir. Has she awoken?" She took one look at Joseph practically on top of Abigail and began to back out.

"It is fine, Sanders. I would like a bath drawn, please." Abigail eased back against the pillows. "Mr. Fox was just about to leave."

"Yes, please come in and attend to her ladyship's bath. It appears she is feeling quite a bit better." Bowing slightly to Abigail, he added, "We will continue this conversation at another time, madam."

Abigail resisted the temptation to stick her tongue out at his back.

Chapter Nine

Several weeks later, Abigail pulled on her soft leather gloves and entered Joseph's study. "I am ready to go into town. Is this still a convenient time for you? If not, I could go by myself."

"No. Nothing has changed. You are not to go by yourself. I shall be happy to accompany you. I will have the carriage brought around."

The quick flash of anger in her eyes reminded him she had still not reconciled herself to having his company on all treks into town. Perhaps he was being foolish, and sending a footman with her would suffice, but the gnawing certainty in his mind that the bullet had not been from a careless hunter kept him from taking that step. He'd not have her injured once again. Although, he was also hard pressed to allow that the bullet had been on purpose. Why anyone would purposely shoot at his wife didn't bear consideration.

A conundrum for sure.

She offered him a tight smile. "No need. I've already

asked Manning to have that done."

A smile twitched his lips as he watched her fuss with her gloves, then move to the mirror on the wall across from his desk and adjust her hat, smooth back her hair. He loved watching her when she was unaware of his regard. He still hadn't gotten used to having a wife. Although she hadn't been a wife in the true sense of the word since her injury. But he assured himself enough time had passed, and her healing would be complete. Tonight he would ply her with soft words and perhaps a bit of wine.

His body tightened with anticipation.

They strolled together out of the house and down the steps to the waiting carriage. He assisted Abigail into the conveyance, and grabbing the bar, swung himself onto the seat, settling across from her. The vehicle moved forward to the familiar sound of hooves striking the pebbled pathway.

"I am looking forward to seeing how the school building is progressing," Joseph said as he crossed one booted foot over his knee. "The last time I visited, the workers were already laboring on the inside. We should be able to begin accepting students in a few weeks.

"And I received a note from the book people that our shipment of supplies should arrive shortly. In fact, we might find it has already been delivered to the school."

Abigail gazed out of the window for a few moments, then turned to him. "I should like to teach some of the students myself."

"Indeed? I had no idea you desired to be a governess." He smiled at her affronted look at his teasing.

"Must I tell you once again that I am not the spoiled young debutante that you insist on painting me? In truth, I had grown weary of the constant round of parties and balls that comprise the Season in London. My closet can hold no more gowns, and I have no need for more ribbons, bonnets, and gloves."

She leaned forward, as if to emphasize her sincerity. "I want to do something worthwhile. I have had all the advantages of money and station, and only since I've met your parishioners and their children, do I realize how very fortunate I have been. If I can teach just one child to read and write, and do sums, which will enhance his life, then that would mean more to me than all the ball gowns I possess."

The fire in her eyes seared him. Perhaps he had indeed been thinking that as a duke's sister she would be content with seeing the building raised and the supplies delivered for others to contend with. He knew from experience dealing with children would involve runny noses, soiled hands, and tears tracking down dirty cheeks.

"I apologize if I have hurt your feelings. That was never my intention. You must forgive me my thoughtlessness since, like most of us who are not in the upper classes, we assume, maybe unfairly, that those of you who are, would never delve into a project such as this with all the enthusiasm you offer." He reached across the space separating them and took her hand. "And for that I am grateful to have you as my wife."

• • •

Abigail warmed at his words. Even if he had married her for money, he was a considerate and caring man. If she could only disabuse him of this notion that all she was good for was to sit around and watch everyone else work.

She would certainly prove him wrong. Despite her station, her upbringing had been unusual for members of the *ton*. Her mother had not been one to give birth, then turn over the raising of her children to nannies and governesses. The Dowager Duchess of Manchester had romped in the snow, organized games for the village children, and herded her brood of seven children to many a picnic and trek to the swimming hole.

True, Abigail had never been in a position to have to seek employment, but she was determined to make a go of her situation and since love would never be involved in her marriage, at least she could have the satisfaction of knowing she'd made a difference in someone's life.

The remainder of the ride was spent in pleasant conversation about the school, with Abigail's excitement growing. "How shall we go about enrolling the children?"

"Most likely we will need to make visits to the townspeople's homes. It will be important for us to reassure them that the children will not neglect their household chores. At the same time, we'll need to emphasize the importance of education."

The carriage rolled to a stop in front of the dry goods store, where the mail was delivered. Joseph helped Abigail down, and they entered the store to the sound of a small bell that chimed as the door opened.

"Mr. Fox. I have quite a delivery here for you." The man behind the counter sported a full beard, and a large nose, which somehow balanced out his looks. He pushed his spectacles up on his face and waved in the direction of the rear of the store. "I had the man stack them all in my back room."

"Thank you, Mr. Davies. Those would be the supplies for our school. I should like to take a look at what has arrived."

Mr. Davies led the way through a narrow corridor to a dimly lit back room. He pointed to boxes stacked along the south wall of the building. "There you are, Mr. Fox."

Three rows of boxes, standing about five high, took up a goodly amount of space. Each container was stamped with the words Lumsden & Son.

"May we go through them now?" Abigail asked.

"Perhaps another day when we have more time. In fact, I will arrange for the boxes to be sent to the school building, and we can peruse them at our leisure." Joseph addressed the store owner. "Can you have these delivered to the new school building?"

"Yes, of course, Mr. Fox. As soon as young Charlie is through with his chores at home, I'll have him bring them by in our wagon." The man hesitated for a moment, then continued. "Might I say that I am grateful for your interest in educating our children? Others might think it a waste of time, but I want Charlie and his brothers to take over this store, and as busy as Mrs. Davies and I are, there is really no time to teach them their letters and numbers."

"Thank you, Mr. Davies. That is our aim for this school," Joseph said, as Abigail looked at the selections of soap.

After choosing a bar of rose-scented soap, cream for her hands, and several handkerchiefs for Joseph, Abigail tucked her arm into her husband's and they left the store.

The pale green leaves on the trees lining the winding cobbled street bestowed a sense of newness, along with a resurgence of hope. Early summer always felt like a new beginning. The soft breeze on her face felt like silk, the pale sun warming her skin. She breathed deeply of the honeysuckle climbing a stone fence surrounding a small cottage. She smiled at the resemblance to the drawings in her fairy tale books that her mother had read to them every night during her childhood. A sense of peace, belonging, and joy filled her. She turned to Joseph and caught him staring at her, a slight smile on this face. "What?" she asked.

"I enjoy watching you. You seem content."

She tilted her head, studying him. "I believe I am."

"And is that all you wish for?"

She stiffened, afraid he was looking for more. More than she was prepared to give. "Yes, I believe there is a lot to be said for contentment."

The day suddenly didn't seem quite so rosy. Joseph confused her, caused her to wonder exactly what it was he wanted from her. Their marriage had not only provided him with her dowry, but also freed up his own money. That had been their agreement. He would get the money he needed for his school, she would get the respectability of marriage, home, and one day a family.

She certainly hoped he wasn't planning on changing the rules. She'd made it perfectly clear when he'd proposed. A friendship, a partnership. Fondness perhaps, and yes— contentment. But she had no intention of opening up her heart again.

• • •

Joseph sensed Abigail's withdrawal. He felt as though he were walking on thinly layered ice. It had all seemed so easy at the beginning. Their agreement had made sense. If not for his impromptu visit to Manchester, he would have finished his business in London, and returned with enough donors to build his school. One day he would have taken a wife, but that had certainly not been on his mind that morning.

Now he found himself married to a woman he'd relegated to the back of his mind years ago as unattainable. A woman he could easily fall in love with, if he hadn't already. But she wanted no part of his love.

"Mr. Fox." Joseph was brought out of his musing by a shrill, feminine voice behind him.

He turned to see Lady Durham hurrying toward them, her face flushed. He and Abigail paused to allow her to join them.

"I just heard that you were shot, Lady Abigail. My goodness, how terrible for you. Are you recovered?" Lady Durham took Abigail's hand, her face a mask of concern.

"Yes, I am fine. Thank you, Lady Durham." Abigail smiled warmly.

"Do you have any idea who did this terrible thing?" The woman leaned in farther, causing Abigail to move back a step, bumping into Joseph's chest.

She shrugged. "Most likely a careless hunter."

Lady Durham stepped back with a sigh. "I am so very happy that you are fully recovered. As I'm sure Mr. Fox is." She smiled brightly at him.

"Indeed."

"Well, I shall be on my way. I wish you continued good health, Lady Abigail."

Abigail dipped her head gracefully. "Thank you."

"Yes, thank you for your concern," Joseph added.

• • •

Later that evening, a soft knock on her dressing room door drew Abigail's attention from her place at the window. In the scant moonlight, she could see the well-tended garden with the meandering pathway that continued out of her sight, ending at the orangery. "Yes?"

Joseph entered the room, dressed in a red and brown print banyan. She had realized that he intended to resume lovemaking. If his heated gazes hadn't forewarned her, the constant touches as they sat at dinner, and later in the library while he enjoyed a brandy, had made it perfectly clear that his forced celibacy would come to an end tonight.

He'd been the consummate gentleman while she'd been recovering, solicitous and accommodating. Although they'd slept in the same bed the entire time, he had ended each evening with a kiss to her forehead, and then had rolled over to sleep. Or at least he had given the impression of going to sleep.

With the pain in her arm settling into a constant ache the last few days, it had taken her a while to fall asleep each night. She'd been aware of Joseph's restlessness, his thrashing, and the lengthening of time each night until she heard his deep breathing.

"You look particularly lovely this evening." He sauntered toward her, the banyan separating as he neared, drawing her eyes to his muscular legs, dusted in brown hair. Her stomach clenched with expectation, and her heart sped up. Disconcerted at how much she'd missed his attentions, she reminded herself that once she found herself with child, she would insist he uphold his part of their agreement.

But could she?

Joseph stopped a mere few inches from her and cupped her face in his warm, large hands. "I've missed you."

"I haven't been gone." Her attempt to bring levity into their exchange faltered when her voice came out raspy and breathless. Good heavens, his mere touch weakened her knees so that she needed to grab onto his arms to keep herself upright. His strong arms, warm and firm, the muscles shifting under her palms as he moved his hands down, pulled her closer.

He leaned his forehead on hers. "I want you so much, but I'm concerned for your injury." He scattered kisses along her jaw, her neck and the sensitive skin behind her ear. "Please tell me you've healed enough."

"Yes." She moaned softly, and slid her hand up, her fingers tangling in his hair. "I believe I have."

"Thank the Lord." Suddenly, she was lifted into the cradle of his arms, and he strode to the bed, laying her gently down, then stretching out alongside her. "If I hurt you, please let me know."

She hummed her answer and pulled his head down for a searing kiss. All thoughts of pain, keeping Joseph from her bed once she was with child, and life in general, seeped from her mind as his roving hands left a trail of fire in their wake.

Sliding her nightgown from her shoulders, he blazed a trail of kisses from her collarbone to her navel before moving up her body, nibbling on her skin. His tongue caressed her sensitive swollen nipple, and he suckled hard—she felt the pull all the way to her core.

He raised his head and stared into her eyes, his hand drifting over her curves. "I love the feel of your skin under my hands. It's like silk. I could do this all day." His eyes darkened, a fine sheen of perspiration covering his body. His hand moved to her lower back, and he eased her close, rubbing himself against her core.

The strength of his body robbed her of breath. She brushed the hair back from his brow, wondering what it was she saw in his eyes. Hunger—absolutely. He desired her, there was no doubt. But something else in his look frightened her. The tenderness, the longing for what he wanted from her that wasn't only physical. Something she would forever hold back.

His gaze drifted to her lips. Her concerns forgotten for the moment, her entire world narrowed to Joseph's mouth and hands. She was enveloped in his scent, the heaviness of his body pressing her into the mattress. He shifted, his fingers playing at the entrance to her body, sliding in and out of her feminine heat.

After several minutes of this torture, Abigail's body tensed as she reached for the ultimate pleasure that she knew only he could give her. Her legs moved restlessly, she pressed against his hand. "Please."

"As you wish, sweetheart," he whispered into her ear, running his tongue around the delicate shell. His knee edged her legs apart, and within seconds he slid into her. Her eyes drifted closed at the fullness that filled her body and soul.

No!

She couldn't allow her soul to be part of this. It was the satisfaction she desired, the waves of pleasure that she knew would wash over her.

Joseph braced himself on his elbows above her, leaning his forehead down to touch hers. His breath was warm on her face and smelled of the brandy he'd had. She licked her lips and he groaned, anchoring her head with his hands, and took her mouth in a possessive kiss.

She moved in rhythm with him, reaching, stretching, striving for her release. The sound of their panting filled the room, their bodies, slippery with passion, moved together as if they'd practiced this dance for years.

Within minutes, Abigail tightened her leg muscles as wave after wave of pleasure flowed over her. Before the last wave left, Joseph threw his head back and growled as he gave one final thrust.

He collapsed alongside of her, careful of her wound. She moved her arm to run her fingers over his back, her muscles no stronger than water. Joseph mumbled something into her neck, but she was drifting off to sleep before his words ended.

• • •

Abigail had been sleeping soundly for more than an hour, snuggled up against Joseph's side as he lay awake, studying the canopy over his head.

He was in love with his wife.

Instead of the glorious feelings that should have brought him, he wrestled with the knowledge that she would never love him back.

Could he spend the rest of his life loving a woman who would always hold him at arm's length? Who he would always suspect wished another man in his place?

A rush of determination gripped him. He'd never been a man to accept what fate had thrown in his path. In this case, fate had provided him with the wife of which he had only dreamed. Whatever it took, he *would* win her love.

Chapter Ten

Joseph held Abigail's chair as she took her seat at the table. Sun shone through the floor-to-ceiling windows, lighting the breakfast room as if a thousand candles burned. The cheerful room always lifted her spirits when she entered. Even on gloomy days, the lack of trees outside the windows allowed sufficient light.

Her insides tightened as she cast him a fleeting glance to gauge his mood. Hopefully, their shared pleasure hadn't encouraged Joseph to believe their relationship would change. Was she foolish to believe they could share their bodies and the pleasure it brought them, and still remain no more than friends?

Many *ton* marriages were no more than business arrangements, with husband and wife producing the needed heir and spare before they went their separate ways. They would live in the same house, share meals and occasional entertainments, but mistresses and lovers were common.

It was the type of marriage she'd always scorned, since her parents had had a love match as did her brother, Drake. She and her sisters had been adamant about waiting for a man they loved and who would love them back.

How ridiculous she'd been.

Joseph pushed his empty plate away and took a sip of his coffee. "What are your plans for today?"

"I thought perhaps a trip into town to open the boxes that were delivered yesterday?"

"Of course I want to join you, but I have a tutoring session this morning. Can you find something to keep busy with until after luncheon?"

"Yes. I wanted to meet with the gardener to go over some plans I have for the area behind the orangery. That is, if it meets with your approval."

"This is your home now, Abigail. You may do as you see fit."

Her home. An odd little jolt of pleasure shot through her. "Thank you. Then shall we plan on a trip into town this afternoon?"

Again that smile. "Yes."

She excused herself and left the room to gather her gloves and bonnet from her bed chamber.

Once outside, Abigail breathed deeply of the warm fragrant air as she headed toward the garden. Tying the wide ribbons of her bonnet under her chin, she wandered the path in search of Edward, the gardener. Despite being the only employee to care for the grounds, the area was well tended, the flowers in full bloom.

The sun beat down, causing beads of perspiration to form on her forehead and upper lip. Earthy scents, mixed with the enticing aroma of honeysuckle and roses, followed her as she strolled the herbaceous gardens. Enjoying the morning, she allowed her thoughts to wander.

Joseph was a considerate man, and a generous lover who made sure of her pleasure, allowing for her inexperience. When she thought of the years she had spurned completely acceptable suitors because she wanted love, it all seemed rather childish. Love, indeed. Fairy tales her mother had read to her and her sisters as children.

It mattered not that her brother had found love with his wife. She shoved to the back of her mind the image of how they gazed upon each other. Almost as if they spoke a silent language known only to them. Well, she and Joseph would have a mature marriage. A relationship built on common goals, respect, and perhaps even affection.

One day, there would be a child or two for them to shower their love upon. Of course, if she planned to ban him from her bed after she conceived, there would only be the one child. Perhaps when she decided the time was right for another child, she would sensibly and in a very sophisticated manner advise him that he could resume visiting her bed. Yes, it would work well.

Satisfied at her plan for how their marriage would go on, she picked up her pace and headed to the back of the orangery where she spotted someone rounding the corner of the building, most likely Edward.

She turned the corner and came to an abrupt halt. The gardener was nowhere in sight. Funny, that. She was almost certain she'd seen someone. She placed her hands on her hips and turned in a circle to survey the area.

The heavy door to the garden shed swayed in the breeze.

Perhaps he'd gone in there to fetch something. Swiping her hand across her forehead, she continued on.

"Edward?" she called from outside the shed.

Only the slight creak of the door as it swung back and forth acknowledged her. She stepped into the garden shed, the coolness of the space a welcomed relief. Blinking several times in an effort to see more clearly, she picked her way down the aisle with shelves of tools and other garden implements arranged on the walls.

Despite the spaciousness of the garden shed, it was obvious to her restored vision that Edward wasn't here. She jerked and swung around when the heavy wooden door slammed shut, the sound echoing in her ears. The scant light from the doorway disappeared, leaving her with a feeling of being trapped, without enough air. Strange, it had hardly seemed windy enough to cause the door to slam shut.

There didn't seem to be any point in lingering here, and truth be known, the darkness and confinement made her uneasy. She made her way carefully to the door and pushed, surprised to find it immovable. Leaning her shoulder against the worn wood, she gave it a good shove, and only managed to hurt herself. She stepped back and studied the door while she rubbed her arm.

Drat! The latch must have fallen when the door slammed shut. A quick glance around the garden shed confirmed no windows. She tamped down her rising panic at being trapped. The building was far enough away from the house that she could pound all day and unless someone was right outside, they wouldn't hear her. She put her lips to the crack between the door and the doorjamb. "Help!"

That was when the pungent odor of smoke drifted to

her nostrils.

• • •

Distracted from his paperwork, Joseph checked his timepiece once again. The mother of the young man he tutored had sent a note around that he had contracted a chill and would remain at home for the morning. With the extra time on his hands, he decided to tend to some of his correspondence, but his thoughts kept wandering to Abigail.

He turned in his chair and studied the beautiful morning outside. Sunlight poured through the leaves on the large oak tree outside his window, casting dappled patterns on the lush summer grass. A slight breeze ruffled the honeysuckle bursting forth along the pebbled pathway. Bright sunny days were not all that common in England, so perhaps he should dispense with his paperwork, and join Abigail outdoors.

Edward came into his view as he pushed a wheelbarrow from the direction of the garden shed to the small vegetable garden Cook used to grow herbs. Any minute he expected to see Abigail join him to go over her plans for the garden.

When she didn't appear, he rotated his shoulder muscles to ease the tension from sitting at the desk, and resumed reading his letters. After realizing he'd read the same paragraph three times, he dropped the paper back on the desk and turned once more toward the window.

Edward was on his knees, but Abigail still had not joined him. Perhaps she'd already concluded her business and decided to enjoy the fine weather with a stroll. As he watched the gardener work, the man suddenly stood, and raising his hand to block the sun from his eyes, stared off into the distance. He leaned in farther, then turned toward the back door of the house. Cupping his hands around his mouth, he shouted something Joseph didn't hear. The man then took off running toward the direction he'd been studying.

A knot of fear settled in Joseph's stomach. He bolted from his chair and strode to the door. Within seconds he'd reached the end of the corridor and flung open the back door.

Smoke billowed up from behind the orangery. The only structure back there was the garden shed, which Edward would have been able to see from his position in the garden. The kernel of fear spread, leaving his heart pounding.

"Fire!" Edward's second shout had Joseph running down the stairs and leaping over flowers as he crisscrossed the garden, ignoring the footpath. He turned the corner of the orangery to see flames licking the front of the shed. Edward was hauling a bucket of water from the well. His two footmen ran up and they quickly formed a line.

"Abigail!" Joseph roared, looking frantically around.

She was nowhere in sight, and he hadn't passed her in his race from the house. It was possible she had gone back inside before he'd left, but every nerve in his body screamed that she was trapped in the shed.

"Abigail!" Once more he bellowed, but she didn't appear.

"Edward, have you seen Abigail yet this morning?" Joseph asked, his voice breathless from panic and his sprint from the house.

The gardener didn't stop tossing water on the garden shed as he answered. "No, sir. Not this morning."

Good God, she's in that shed.

Everything inside his body came to a screeching halt as fear slammed into him, almost bringing him to his knees. Then, spurred by energy he'd never before possessed, he quickly scanned the structure, trying to decide the best way to get her out. He couldn't get in through the front door since it was still engulfed in flames, which were starting to spread to the south wall of the shed.

"Edward, I need an axe," he shouted.

"Near the woodpile at the end of the garden," the gardener yelled as he tossed another bucket of water on the flames.

With no windows to climb through, he had to break into one of the walls before the entire structure went up in flames. Fortunately the garden shed was quite old, and although sturdy, years of weather had taken its toll on the wood.

Joseph dashed to the woodpile and retrieved the axe. Sweat poured down his face and his heart pounded in his ears as he drew back with a growl and slammed the axe into the back of the shed, as far away from the fire as he could get. He would tear the whole damn thing down with his hands if he had to in order to get Abigail out.

He tugged the axe out and struck the wall again. The wood splintered, but the opening was not large enough to fit through. Roaring like a wounded animal, he struck with the axe one more time, then dropped it to smash the wall with his shoulder. "Abigail!" He pushed the broken pieces out of the way and climbed in.

Smoke curled upward, momentarily blinding him. He covered his mouth with his forearm and blinked as tears ran down his face from his burning eyes. "Abigail!"

The shout had dragged smoke into his lungs. He doubled over and began to cough. He wiped his face with this shirt sleeve, and then got down on his hands and knees. With coughs racking his body, he eased down on his belly, keeping as low to the ground as he could, where the air was a bit clearer. Using his elbows, he started down the aisle and spotted her lying on her stomach, her arms over her head as if to protect herself.

With a grunt of relief he inched over to her. Using her shoulders, he rolled her onto her back. Taking a gulp of the cleaner air, he held his breath and hooked his hands under her arms.

Smoke poured from the gaping hole he'd created in the wall. He headed straight for it, dragging Abigail along, the opening like a beacon in the darkness. Once he reached the wall, he bent and scooped her up. Her arms and legs hung down, her head tilted back as if she were unconscious. Turning his back to the hole, he climbed through, holding her snug against his chest to keep her from scraping against the splintered opening. Pieces of broken wood grazed along his sides, tearing his shirt and digging into his skin.

The fresh air was a balm to his body. He inhaled deeply which started another spasm of coughing. He dropped to his knees on the grass as far away from the garden shed as he could carry her before his own breathing difficulties stopped him from walking.

Still struggling for air, he brushed the hair back from her face, cupped her chin, and shook her. Her face was blackened, but she appeared to be breathing. "Abigail." Coughing overtook him once more. "Sweetheart, please open your eyes." His raspy breath scratched his throat.

Abigail took one long shuddering breath and rolled to her side, doubling over as she began to cough. He sat her up and raised her hands above her head. Tears ran down her cheeks, tracking white lines over her soot covered cheeks as she strained to get air into her lungs. Her coughing continued, her face turning red under the black. Gripping her middle, she leaned over and lost the contents of her stomach.

His breathing a bit easier, Joseph pulled his handkerchief from his pocket and wiped her mouth with a shaky hand. Her eyes were bloodshot, soot covered her face, and she continued to cough as if her lungs wanted to escape her body. Yet she had never looked so beautiful to him. He'd almost lost her, and that thought nearly crushed him.

She waved in the direction of the shed. "Still burning." Then she was overtaken with a bout of coughing.

"I don't give a *damn* about the shed. I was only concerned with you." He was so angry at having found her collapsed on the floor of the burning garden shed he didn't even apologize for his language. He longed to take her into his arms and hold her tight, but she still struggled to breathe. His forehead beaded at the thought of how close he had come to losing her. Again.

Right now he needed to get her into the house and out of her smoke filled clothing. She needed a bath and some tea. Or a shot of brandy.

As did he.

Behind them came the sound of the burning structure collapsing. A loud groan emanated from the building as the walls fell inward, sparks and flames rising into the sky. On wobbly legs, he surveyed the damage. His three men continued to toss water on the now smoldering pile.

"Cease." He waved at the men. "Let it burn out."

"Joseph." Abigail's weak cry brought his attention back to her.

He hunkered down and cupped her face, using his thumbs to wipe her tears. Her coughing had eased, but she still took in short, unsteady breaths. "I was so frightened."

"I know, sweetheart. As was I." He pressed her face to his chest, tangling his fingers in her hair, rubbing her scalp. He pushed to the back of his mind any thoughts of how the fire started, and why Abigail was trapped inside. He felt her body shudder as she tried to get fresh air into her lungs.

"Oh my goodness, sir. Whatever happened here?" Mrs. O'Neill hurried over, wiping her hands on her apron, taking in the burned garden shed and Abigail gasping in his arms.

"Mrs. O'Neill, please see that baths are readied for both my wife and myself. Then please prepare some tea for Lady Abigail."

Doing something—anything—to get his mind off the possibility of what could have happened, calmed him. Freed his mind to focus on what he needed to do to help his wife. He gathered Abigail in his arms and stood. She wrapped her arms around his neck as another fit of coughing took her. Without a backward glance at the smoking rubble, he headed to the house.

Joseph stumbled, his body weakened from the strain of the morning events, as he reached their bedchamber. Sanders rushed into the room right on his heels. "Sir, please let me help my lady out of her clothes."

"No."

The maid jerked at his sharp tone. Perhaps he was slowly losing his mind, but he didn't want anyone touching

Abigail, except him. Right now he trusted no one. Although he couldn't imagine who would want to hurt his wife, this was one accident too many. Once she was bathed, and safely ensconced in bed with a tray of tea, he would question her.

"Sanders, please fetch a nightgown for her ladyship and lay it out. We will need some of her soap and warm towels. I will attend to her."

The young maid appeared scandalized. "Sir?"

"Just do as I say, please." Still holding Abigail, he turned toward the door as a footman carried in the large tub, followed by a maid and another footman carrying buckets of water. Abigail whimpered when he tried to release her, so he sat on the daybed across from the fireplace and continued to hold her until the tub was filled, Sanders had laid out a nightgown, and the door had quietly closed.

"Sweetheart?"

She shook her head, bringing a smile to his lips since she looked so much like a stubborn child. "Come on, love. Up we go." He rose and released her legs so she had no choice but to stand. Gripping her hands in his, he backed up and studied her. "I need to get your clothes off so you can bathe."

Nodding, she remained perfectly still as he removed her clothing, tossing them into a pile that he would have Sanders throw away. The stench of the smoke would never leave the garments. Once she was naked, he again scooped her up and carried her to the tub. Easing her into the warm water, he watched as she sighed and leaned her head back, her eyes closed.

He removed his cravat, jacket and waistcoat, then rolled his sleeves up to his elbows. He'd have to get rid of his garments as well. Noting his soot-covered hands, he swished them in the water and gave them a quick wash.

She looked so small, so vulnerable. He rubbed the bar of scented soap over the cloth and removed the grime from her face. She opened her eyes, a haunted look in their depths that twisted his insides. "May I have a drink of water?"

"Of course." He handed her the cloth and crossed the room to the pitcher of water on the table next to their bed. He filled a glass and returned to her. "Here, sweetheart, but don't drink it too fast."

"Thank you." She sipped the liquid, closing her eyes as the water slid down her throat.

Once more the fear that had struck him when he'd first seen the garden shed on fire and had realized that Abigail was in there, gripped him. She could have died, right here in the safety of their own property. How she came to be in the shed, and the place on fire, was something he would investigate thoroughly...later.

For now, he only wanted to hold onto her.

An hour later, they were both bathed and lying in bed, wrapped in each other's arms. Abigail had finished her tea, and he'd downed more than his normal quantity of brandy. The ordeal of the morning had taken its toll and after very few words, both of their throats being somewhat sore, Joseph started to drift off to sleep.

His eyes half-closed, he ran his finger down Abigail's soft cheek. She smelled of flowers and sunshine. All the odor of smoke had left the room with their clothes. Her thick braid rested over one shoulder, and her breathing had the soft and gentle pattern of deep slumber.

She'd changed his life in the short time they'd been married. Just the thought of losing her, of never again seeing her beautiful face first thing in the morning, or last thing at night, terrified him. Somewhere along the way she'd become very important to him. To his life, his very existence.

He continued to study her, more grateful than he could ever express that she was here, next to him, alive and well. Tomorrow—when the horror of today was behind them—they would talk about the fire. Another accident? Not likely, but the alternative, that someone was trying to harm Abigail, was too much to contemplate. He leaned over and kissed her on the forehead.

Sleep well, my love.

Chapter Eleven

"You want to go to London?" Abigail rested in bed, propped against two pillows. Joseph sat on the bed, causing the mattress to dip. He was fully dressed in buckskin breeches, with a blue jacket over a cream-colored waistcoat. His cravat was starched and expertly tied. He'd apparently been up for some time.

She had just awakened from a night of fitful slumber. Dreams had invaded her sleep about flames and being trapped behind them, with Joseph on the other side, calling her, but unable to breach the distance.

It had been near dinner time the night before when they'd awoken from their nap after the terror of the fire. They shared a tray in their room, neither of them wanting to dress and go down to dinner. He'd said very little about the fire, assuring her she needed to rest, and they would discuss it on the morrow. Despite her nap, she'd barely had the energy to finish her dinner. Soon after the tray had been removed, he'd tucked her in, kissed her on the forehead and had left the room to attend to some business in his study.

She'd awoken several times in the night, shaking and gulping air. Each time Joseph had held her and whispered words of comfort. She'd clung to him, chagrined at the raw need to feel his arms around her. For his strength and warmth. Were she able to crawl inside his body she would have.

In the light of day, she was able to push that memory to the back of her mind.

His voice interrupted her musings, drawing her attention back to her question. "Yes, I need to take care of some business, and it would be a good opportunity for a visit with your family."

"But what about your duties here? We have the building of the school to supervise. You have students to tutor and services on Sunday."

"I directed a note to my father last evening, and he is sending a curate from his church to oversee things for a while."

"For a while? How long do you plan for us to be gone?"

"I don't know. Not too long, though. I thought you would be thrilled to see London again."

"Oh, Joseph, you are still under the impression that I miss all of that." She shook her head. "When we discussed our arrangement I thought I'd made it clear. I no longer want that sort of a life. Not that I didn't enjoy it, but after three years, I want more than gowns, balls, and parties."

"Yet, had your marriage to Redgrave gone forward, that is precisely the life you would have had."

Funny how that thought hadn't crossed her mind before

now. Would she have grown bored with *ton* life? Her mother had been involved with society for years. But she'd also spent a great deal of time at their country estate where she'd romped with her seven children.

Redgrave had impressed upon her more than once that he detested living in the country and was satisfied to have his steward take care of his estate while he stayed in Town. He'd also stated that an heir and a spare was all he expected to ever need. When she'd mentioned her parents and their large, loving family, he'd smirked as if she were a silly child. Why hadn't she disputed this? Strange that, at the time, his comments had never bothered her.

Considering them now, they made the man appear frivolous and shallow. Which was exactly what he'd turned out to be. It was difficult not to compare him to Joseph, who was devoting his life to helping others. Her husband's love of children had spurred his concern about their education. Feeling uneasy with the comparison and not sure what to do with those thoughts, she quickly dismissed them.

She drew herself up. "I don't wish to dwell upon the past."

Joseph's smile faltered. "Of course not. Please excuse my bad manners."

Now she'd hurt his feelings. She tried to smooth over her blunder by smiling brightly. "When shall we leave?"

"I thought I'd give you today to rest and prepare yourself. I've notified Sanders of our trip, so she is doing whatever it is that maids do when their ladies travel."

Abigail thrust the covers aside and swung her legs over the edge of the bed. "In that case, I had best speak with her." She faltered when she stood, surprised at the dizziness that washed over her.

Joseph rushed to her side. "Are you all right?" He wrapped his arm around her waist, studying her with concerned eyes.

"I don't know. How strange. I never swoon."

He eased her back on the bed. "Perhaps you need more time to recover from yesterday. Shall I put off our trip?"

"No. I most likely rose too quickly." She patted his hand. "I'll be fine."

He studied her for a moment and then crossed the room. "I will send in Sanders. Should you change your mind and wish to delay the trip for a day or so, merely send word. I will be in my study, going over a few things."

• • •

Joseph closed the study door and wandered to the window. He stood with his hands behind his back in the very spot where he'd seen Edward race for the burning gardener's shed yesterday morning.

Something was wrong, and he didn't know how to go about fixing it. Hence the reason for a trip to London. He had to speak with Drake, get his perspective on this. Abigail had been involved in three mishaps since she'd arrived in Addysby End. The first one had, indeed, been an accident with the Dinger's pig. But the gunshot and burning gardener's shed left him with an uncomfortable feeling.

He hadn't had a chance to question Abigail as yet. She'd been sleeping on and off since the fire. But earlier this morning, he'd discovered that the latch to the gardener's shed door had been secured from the outside. It was possible the wind had blown the door closed with such force that the latch had engaged, however, to his recollection, there had been only a soft breeze yesterday.

He pounded his fist against the window frame in frustration. Abigail had taken it quite well when she'd been shot, but the thought of someone purposely harming her was enough to cripple him. Tomorrow when they took the carriage to London, they would have a long talk. She might hold a clue as to what had happened, but he didn't want to alarm her. It was best if he dealt with his concerns by himself.

It might become necessary for him to leave her at Manchester House in London for a while. But how in heaven's name could he explain to her brother that his sister, whom he'd given him to protect and cherish, had been the victim of multiple injuries in such a short time?

The more difficult issue—one that he hadn't spent too much time considering—was if these happenings were not accidents, who wished Abigail harm?

And why?

. . .

Joseph climbed in alongside Abigail in the well-sprung coach that would take them to London. The skies were heavy with threatened rain, and the air cool for summer. They'd managed to get an early start, which would allow them to reach London by the next day.

"May I say you look particularly lovely today, my dear?"

Abigail wore a blue carriage gown edged with deep blue trim and a matching bonnet. The frock seemed too big. Had she had lost weight while in his care? No surprise, considering what she'd been through since her arrival.

She tugged on her gloves and smiled. "Thank you. Although I truly don't miss the hustle and bustle of London, I am looking forward to visiting with my family."

"Good. I want you to relax and enjoy the journey." Her voice was still a bit raspy. The haunted look had left her eyes, but there remained tension in her face, as if she expected bad news. He hated the feeling of helplessness that evoked. He wanted to make Abigail happy, to give her a life that, if not what she'd planned for, at least made her content. She deserved a husband who adored her, and lively children to smother with the abundance of love she possessed. Love he intended to have her one day cast in his direction, despite her determination to remain apart from those feelings.

Sitting quietly alongside him, his wife studied the landscape as the coach started with a jerk and then smoothed into the familiar sound of horses' hooves striking the ground and the squeak of the carriage wheels turning. As much as he hated to bring up her latest debacle, he had to get to the bottom of her accidents.

Joseph reached out and took Abigail's hands in his, kissing her knuckles. "We need to speak about the fire."

Immediately her body stiffened, and her eyes closed briefly. She licked her lips and took a deep breath. "Yes, I know." She squeezed his hands. "You needn't look so anxious. I can speak of it now."

"I am feeling quite the cad for having brought you to a place that has been so unwelcoming."

She shook her head. "Do not blame yourself. I am sure it's merely a run of bad luck."

He turned her hands over and rubbed his thumb across

the soft skin on the inside of her wrist. "I need to know exactly what happened. How you came to be locked in the shed."

For a minute, despite her assurances that she could speak of it, he feared she would refuse. Her breathing increased, and she worried her lower lip so that he expected to see blood. "There is really nothing strange about that. As I mentioned at breakfast that morning, I wanted to seek out Edward to discuss my plans for the garden." She moved her gaze from him and stared out the window at the passing scenery.

"I thought I saw him walk around the back of the orangery. I assumed he had gone to the shed. When I got there, the door was open, so I called to him from outside. When he didn't answer, I went inside and called him again."

"Did you take the lantern that hung outside the garden shed so you could see better?"

"No." She furrowed her brow. "I wasn't even aware one hung there. I could see far enough in with the light from the open door. I took several steps inside, looked around and then the door slammed behind me." She paled, no doubt at the memory of being enclosed in darkness.

Abigail took a deep breath. "I then found it hard to see, so I turned in what I hoped was the right direction to the door. I tried to open it, but it became apparent that when it had slammed shut, the latch had engaged." She looked down at their joined hands. "It was when I shouted for help that I smelled the smoke."

Without conscious thought he encircled her waist with his hands and pulled her onto his lap. At first, she stiffened, and then relaxed against him, laying her head on his shoulder.

He wrapped her in his arms and held her close, inhaling her scent, feeling her softness. His gut twisted at how close he'd come to losing her.

Quite possibly the slamming of the door had caused the lantern to fall and spill oil onto the door. But the question remained as to how the oil had been ignited. Unwilling to distress her further, Joseph just held her, running his palm up and down her arm, wishing to never let her go.

· · ·

The next afternoon they arrived at the outskirts of London, passing through the worst parts of the city. The housing was poor and bursting with criminals and diseased prostitutes. The effect was one of a densely populated area of gloomy, narrow streets and stark ugliness.

Abigail shivered, hating this part of the trip when returning from the country. Her heart began to thump wildly when a man approached the carriage, running alongside it, begging for money. Joseph snapped the curtain closed and reached under the seat for his pistol.

"Heavens, you won't shoot the man?"

Joseph used his finger to hold part of the curtain open, keeping his eye on their surroundings. "Not as long as he keeps his distance."

She shivered, wishing herself through the streets as quickly as possible. The carriage seemed to speed up, their driver apparently as anxious to leave the area as they were. Within ten minutes they'd left the sordid world behind and had entered the shopping district.

Fashionable ladies strolled along, their maids and

footmen following behind, carrying boxes and bundles. Abigail smiled at the familiar scene, feeling as though she'd been away for months instead of only several weeks.

Soon most of the *ton* would be leaving the stench and heat of the city and heading to their summer homes. Had she not accepted Joseph's offer, she would be returning to Manchester Manor as an unwed and abandoned woman— very close to being on the shelf.

Her gaze slid toward him. More at ease now, since they'd entered the business part of town, he'd returned his pistol to its place. The sun peeking between the clouds streamed through the windows of the carriage, bathing his face in sunlight. His hair needed a trim, the dark ends curling over the back of his cravat. He rested his chin on his index finger and thumb, staring out the window, apparently deep in thought.

Her husband.

The man who had saved her from yet another Season. Who had promised from the Book of Common Prayer to *love her, comfort her, honor, and keep her in sickness and in health; forsaking all other…*

How many weddings had she attended and heard the same words repeated? And so few of the matches had involved love. Yet everyone sat in still quietude and listened to the bride and groom promise to do such before God, when most marriages were merely a convenience. Like hers.

It hurt to think that Joseph might regret the hurried wedding. Not that he'd ever given her any reason to believe so. As a true gentleman, he wouldn't. But she had been so focused on what she would and would not grant him as his wife, she'd never thought to ask if he'd had someone in mind to make an offer for. The thought of her selfishness horrified her.

.   "Joseph, I know it is a bit late to ask this, but had you someone already in mind to marry before my brother talked you into this arrangement?"

He graced her with that slow half smile that always went directly to her middle. "Indeed, it is a bit too late to ask that question." His eyelids grew heavy and he reached his hand out. "Come here." She rose from her seat and settled on his lap. He brushed back an errant curl that had escaped her bonnet. His deep brown eyes appeared to look right into her soul. "Nowhere on this earth is there anyone else to whom I would prefer to be married."

Slowly his head descended, his lips covering hers. The kiss was long and thorough, his tongue teasing her lips until she opened and he swept in. Small butterflies took flight in her stomach, spreading upward, setting her heart to thumping, and her breathing to hitch.

Joseph slid his hand down and covered her breast, kneading the soft flesh, his thumb circling her nipple until it hardened, causing a slight moan to escape her lips. He released her mouth and scattered kisses along her jaw, moving to the soft skin behind her ear where he nibbled, then soothed.

Abigail lost all appreciation for time and place, her senses alive with longing, wanting more of Joseph's touches, his clever hands, his talented mouth.

He pulled back, his eyes darkened with passion, as he rubbed the pad of his thumb over her swollen lips. "We must stop. Soon we will be at Manchester House. It would not do well for Manchester to see his sister arrive disheveled and breathless." He winked at her as he righted her clothing, then drew her to him. She curled into his body, resting her head on his chest.

As she lay cuddled in his arms, she realized he hadn't answered her question.

Chapter Twelve

They had barely alighted from the carriage when her sister-in-law, Penelope, hurried down the stairs, her arms outstretched. "How wonderful of you to visit." She hugged Abigail, then turned to Joseph. "We were so happy to get your note that you were arriving today."

Joseph bowed and took Penelope's hand. "Your Grace, you are looking splendid as always."

Penelope beamed at them both, then looped her arm through Abigail's and walked her up the steps. Joseph followed, both anxious and relieved to be able to discuss his concerns with Drake. "Is His Grace at home?"

"Oh, for heaven's sake," Abigail said, turning toward him. "You and Drake were in leading strings together. If you refer to him as 'His Grace' his head will get bigger than it already is."

She laughed and leaned close to Penelope. "Has Drake ever told you about the time he and Joseph tied me to a tree to keep me from following them?"

"Yes, he did. And I told him what I thought of that."

Abigail laughed. "I'm embarrassed to say it was well deserved. I used to traipse behind them everywhere they went."

Penelope looked at Joseph. "To answer your question, yes, Drake is at home, and will join us in the drawing room as soon as he finishes with his secretary, Miles." She released Abigail's arm to allow the butler to relieve them of their hats and gloves.

"First, I imagine you would like to refresh yourselves in your room."

"Yes, I believe I would." Abigail and Joseph followed Penelope up the stairs. She chatted the entire way, mostly about her son and the amazing progress he was making each day. Joseph was thrilled to know the smartest child ever born resided at Manchester House. With all the babe had accomplished in his short life, he would no doubt be speaking at the House of Lords before he was out of nappies. Joseph grabbed Penelope's elbow as she stumbled on the last step.

She shook her head. "I must speak to Stevens about having these steps repaired."

Joseph and Abigail grinned at each other.

They wandered down the corridor past several rooms until Penelope opened the door to a bedchamber. "I know this is a bit fancy for a gentleman, but I hope you don't mind staying in Abigail's bedchamber."

"Not at all, Your Grace. This is fine."

"Oh please, Joseph. Let us refrain from all formality. We are family. And you certainly know my name."

She fussed for a bit, making sure everything was suitable,

and then left them with instructions to join her and Drake for tea. Once the door closed on the whirlwind that was Penelope, Abigail and Joseph looked at each other and burst into laughter.

Abigail circled the room, dragging her fingers over the furniture, ending at the window where she rested her palm on the window frame and gazed out. "It seems as though I have been away for a very long time."

Joseph came to stand behind her and wrapped his arms around her waist, then settled his chin on her shoulder. "Is that good or bad?"

She shrugged. "Honestly? I don't know." Twisting her neck, she looked at him, her lips close enough to reach his. "The last few weeks in this room were miserable ones, for sure. However…"

He kissed her briefly on her lips. "Life hasn't been much better since then?"

She turned in his arms, her eyes filled with tears. "For the first time in my life I'm afraid."

"Oh, sweetheart." His stomach muscles tightened as though he'd received a punch to the gut. Leaning his forehead against hers, he used his thumbs to wipe the two tears that had escaped and rolled down her cheeks to puddle in her lips. At that moment he was prepared to abandon his parish, forget the school, sell his house, and move as far away from Addysby End as he could get. Cornwall, perhaps.

"You can stay here with your family. I will return home and investigate these matters."

She pulled back and frowned. "What matters?"

Joseph shook his head in confusion. "The accidents you've been having. Isn't that why you say you're afraid?"

"I don't believe the accidents are anything to investigate. I merely feel unsettled and fearful of small spaces and the dark. Things I've never been afraid of before." She swiped at the remaining tears and rested her palms on his chest. "Why would you think an investigation is necessary?"

He didn't know whether to be relieved that she didn't connect the gunshot with the gardener's shed fire, or amazed that she hadn't. Torn between revealing his fears, which might make her more anxious, or keeping them close to his chest which might not be in her best interest, he studied her beautiful face. Which would it be: ignorance or added distress?

It was his responsibility to protect her, although he'd done a poor job of it thus far. No purpose would be served in frightening her further. He would talk with Drake and get his thoughts on it. Perhaps she was right, and there was no reason to assume these were not accidents.

He decided on ignorance.

• • •

Arms linked, Abigail and Penelope strolled in the garden behind Manchester House. With Drake's sisters and the dowager duchess attending a house party in Cheshire, the unfamiliar quiet was both soothing and unnerving. Abigail welcomed the tranquility, but the distraction of her sisters' chatter would have settled her, given her something else to ponder besides her new found fears.

Deciding instead to ask her sister-in-law's advice on another troubling topic, she steered them to the stone bench warmed from the sun. They settled side by side under the shady coolness of a large oak tree. Fragrant honeysuckle and aromatic summer roses from the well-tended garden mixed with a faint breeze to effect a perfect summer afternoon. Two honeybees battled for nectar, drifting from flower to flower, sucking up the sweetness.

The sun on her face and the familiar sights and sounds of summer calmed her. For the first time in days, Abigail felt peace descend. No darkness here, no enclosing walls to cause her breathing to speed up. She sighed with contentment.

"I am so glad to see you relax," Penelope said, also raising her face up to the sun. "I love this garden. Well, actually, I love the outdoors."

"This was always my favorite spot when my family spent time in Town." Abigail glanced over at Penelope and chuckled.

"What?" Penelope said, opening her eyes.

"I'm thinking if Mother saw us both out without our bonnets, and actually encouraging the sun to bathe our faces, we would be dragged back into the house and not allowed out until dark."

Penelope giggled. "Yes, indeed. She is forever admonishing me about the sun. But I'm afraid all my years of wallowing around in the dirt, digging for plant specimens, have already ruined my skin."

"Not at all. Your complexion is lovely."

After a few minutes of silence, Abigail turned to Penelope. "Would it be much too forward of me to ask when you knew you loved my brother?"

Penelope stilled, then slanted a glance at her. "Not an easy answer, I'm afraid."

"Why?"

"Because there was no moment in time when I said, 'I love this man.' You may recall I was quite unsettled during our betrothal." She smiled at the memory. "I was absolutely certain that Drake would soon come to regret his decision to marry me."

"If memory serves, he really had no choice."

"Yes, there is that. But even though we had been caught in a . . . Well, he felt marriage was the only way to salvage the situation. I pleaded with him to cry off, and allow me to return to the country."

"Yet it is obvious to any observer that you adore each other."

A slight blush colored Penelope's cheeks. "Yes."

"Were you ever afraid?"

"Oh, goodness, all the time. I was afraid I would make a cake of myself and embarrass him and your entire family." She raised her chin. "You may not have noticed, but I tend to have unfortunate things happen to me. You know, little mistakes and such."

Abigail struggled to not laugh at her sister-in-law's description of her many stumbles and mishaps. The poor woman could hardly get through a day without some sort of blunder. As frustrated as Drake had been with her at the beginning, he now regarded her with such love that it made Abigail's heart ache to witness it.

"What I meant, though, were you ever afraid of…" She licked her lips. "That is, did it worry you…?"

Penelope took her hand, frowning. "What is it, Abigail?"

"You know I fancied myself in love with Redgrave."

"If that is how you see it. I know you *claimed* to be in love with him."

"Well, perhaps I was not. Perhaps I don't know what love is. Perhaps I am some foolish dreamer who thinks she is in love when she isn't and–"

"And you think you're in love with Joseph, but are afraid?"

Abigail pulled back, started to shake her head in denial, and then slumped. "Yes."

"Ah. What are you afraid of?"

"It is confusing. Suppose I was not in love with Redgrave, but only thought I was? And then he ran off with Lady Priscilla, and I was heartbroken, I believed. But I seemed to recover rather quickly. Is love so fleeting then?"

"No, I don't believe it is. If Drake ran off with someone else—well he wouldn't be Drake, then, would he?" She pondered for a moment, and then added, "I don't suppose that helped you a great deal, did it?"

Abigail reached out and pulled Penelope into a hug. "Yes. Actually you did help. If Redgrave had truly loved me, he wouldn't have run off, and if I had truly loved him, I believe it would have taken me a lot longer to mend."

"Did I say all that?"

"Yes. You did. And now I believe it's time to dress for dinner."

Once more with arms linked, they strolled back to the house. Abigail certainly didn't know why, but she felt better.

• • •

"Can I pour you a brandy?" Drake asked from the sideboard in the drawing room. Joseph nodded and settled on a chair next to a window with a spectacular view of the gardens.

He had just left Abigail in their bedchamber, dressing for dinner.

Drake handed him the drink and took the seat next to him, crossing a booted foot over his knee. "Now that the ladies are otherwise occupied, perhaps you will tell me the real reason for this trip."

Joseph swirled the brown liquid in his glass and studied its movement. They'd been at Manchester House all afternoon. He had hoped to speak to Drake while the ladies had fussed in the nursery, and then when they had taken a leisurely stroll in the garden. But his brother-in-law had been tied up with estate business. Joseph had spent the time making notes on his concerns. Eventually frustrated at how little he knew, he had torn up the paper and fed it to the fireplace.

After leaning against the mantle shelf, watching the notes disappear into ash, he had pulled on his jacket and left the room. A brisk ride on one of Drake's magnificent stallions had left him no more insightful, but less tense.

"I am concerned for Abigail's safety."

A slight hesitation as Drake raised his glass for a sip of his brandy was the only reaction to Joseph's statement. In true Manchester form, he swallowed, then nodded. "Go on."

Joseph laid his glass on a table and stood, the tension he'd lived with the past few days hitting him full force. He ran stiff fingers through his hair, then settled his hands on his hips. "There have been accidents. Two."

"Penelope has 'accidents' all the time." Despite Joseph's anxiety, he was immediately struck by the softening of Manchester's face, and twinkle in his eyes when he spoke of his wife. A longing he'd pushed to the back of his mind rose to the forefront, strengthening his resolve to spend more time wooing his wife once the mystery of her accidents was cleared up.

"Serious accidents," he clarified.

Manchester set his drink down, and leaned forward, his elbows braced on his knees. "Perhaps you'd better start at the beginning."

Joseph paced as he related the events since he and Abigail had arrived in Addysby End. His gut clenched as he again relived the discovery of the bullet wound and the horror of watching the garden shed go up in flames, certain that Abigail was locked inside. He wiped beads of perspiration from his brow, his agitation growing as he spoke.

"And there you have it." He took his seat once more. "I don't at this point think Abigail believes these were outright attempts to harm her. Frankly, I'm not sure if I want her to consider that. Right now she is already fearful of being enclosed as a result of her experience in the shed. As far as I can tell, she hasn't connected that event to the shooting."

"But you have."

"Doesn't it seem likely to you?"

Drake pondered for a minute, the only sound in the room that of the grandfather clock in the corner. Joseph glanced out the window, the scene no longer soothing him. Tension radiated throughout his body, the frustration at his helplessness almost crippling.

"The first question, of course, is if Abigail has gained any enemies in her short time at Addysby End?"

"No. Everyone loves her."

"If what you expect is true, not *everyone* loves her."

Drake's questioning brought to the forefront what

Joseph had been avoiding for weeks. If, indeed, these "accidents" were actually "on purposes," who would be behind such a horrible scheme? As a rector, it was his duty to see the best in people, to forgive mistakes and lapses in behavior and human failures. Now he would be forced to view everyone in a different light. To suspect where perhaps there was no cause.

What a conundrum.

"We've arrived." Penelope and Abigail entered the room in a swirl of colorful silk and muslin.

Joseph was again taken with the picture Abigail presented. Her deep brown eyes settled on him the moment she gained the room. Her hair was piled on her head in a becoming fashion that allowed for it to appear as if she had just arisen from her bed. He felt his groin tighten with the sultry smile she offered.

Her gown, a deep rose with a white panel down the center, showed off her figure charmingly. The cut of her bodice was modest, but with enough daring that her breasts drew his eyes immediately. All that creamy skin plumped above her bodice had his mouth watering. Perhaps they could forego dinner and retire to their bedchamber.

"We will continue our conversation in the morning." Drake spoke *sotto voce* before he ambled across the room to his wife, leaving Joseph to adjust his breeches before he joined Abigail.

Joseph thought the meal would never end. Every time Abigail threw her head back and laughed, exposing all that silky skin, he had broken into a sweat. He had no idea what they had eaten, or if it was as appetizing as Abigail claimed. His mouth had been dry as a desert since she'd swept into the drawing room with Penelope.

He only wanted dessert, and that he would have in the privacy of their bedchamber. However, Penelope suggested since it was only the four of them, they might dispense with separating after dinner, with the men staying for brandy, and the ladies retreating for tea. So they all trooped into the drawing room where the tea cart stood.

Things also dragged on when Nanny brought the heir from the nursery to spend time with his parents before bed. The infant was the light of his parents' life, but to Joseph he was merely a funny looking creature. And an obstacle to his dessert. Although, had the child been his and Abigail's, surely he would be the most interesting of babes and easy to gaze upon for hours.

Finally, Nanny fetched the child, and Penelope and Drake rose, hand-in-hand, and announced their intentions to retire for the evening. Based on the looks between the two, they intended to enjoy a bit of dessert themselves.

"Shall we, my dear?" Joseph extended his arm to Abigail. They strolled up the stairs and down the corridor to their bedchamber. Once inside, Joseph dismissed Sanders, intending to be Abigail's lady's maid for the night.

"I must say it feels rather odd to have a man in my bedchamber." Abigail stopped in the center of the space, then pivoted, taking in her childhood room.

Joseph moved behind her and pressed a kiss to the soft skin at her nape; skin that had been driving him crazy all evening. "Not just a man, sweetheart, your husband."

She turned and rested her palms on his shoulders. "What were you and Drake so somberly discussing when Penelope and I came down this evening?"

The very last thing he wanted was to distract Abigail from his intentions. Or know the depth of his concern. So he used the best method of distraction he knew. Slowly he lowered his head and murmured, "Nothing as important as this."

His lips covered hers with a possession that stunned him. He wrapped his arms around her waist, holding her snug against his body as he felt her knees sag. She was warm, soft, and smelled of flowers. He nudged her lips open and swept his tongue into her mouth, tasting the sweetness from the tea she'd had. She tangled with him, the duel of tongues causing his blood to race.

"My God, you're so beautiful. I want to strip you bare and kiss every inch of your skin." He pulled back and spun her, quickly unfastening the buttons of her gown.

"Be careful, this is new," Abigail panted.

"I'll buy you three more."

The gown dropped to the floor, leaving her in her chemise and stays. He made quick work of the stays. Once they fell free of her body, he pushed the chemise down until she remained in all her glorious nakedness, her garments pooled at her feet.

Joseph cupped her breasts and gazed through half-lidded eyes over her shoulder at his hands, dark against her milky skin. Her cheeks were flushed, and her hair had almost fallen completely down. A quick flick of his fingers and the remaining hairpins flew from her head, the pinging noise mixing with their heavy breaths.

Her hair felt like silk as he ran his fingers through it, inhaling its scent. Abigail moved her hand behind her and fingered his length, pressing her shoulders to his chest giving rise to her breasts as she slid her hand up and down. If he didn't get her into bed soon he'd end up taking her right here on the floor like some strumpet. "Sweetheart, let's get into bed."

She turned and brushed the hair off his forehead, then ran her fingers down his cheek, to his jaw, then his chest. Her eyes darkened with passion, she dropped to her knees and unfastened the placket on his breeches. He stared at the top of her head, his breath completely stolen from his lungs. "What...?" His voice was ragged, his heart pumping so hard he thought it would jump from his chest. Surely she wouldn't...

Joseph fisted her hair and groaned as she kissed him in a place he had never imagined his wife's lips. He had to be causing her pain as he continued to tug on her hair, every muscle in his body tightened, every drop of his blood racing toward only one spot. She trailed her tongue over his member, then drew back and looked up at him, grinning as if she'd found a prize. He almost disgraced himself.

"Sweetheart, please." He bent and lifted her, striding to the bed as he reclaimed her lips, crushing her to him. He laid her down, probably not too gently, given how she bounced. She removed her slippers, but he stopped her before she rolled down her stockings. "Leave them on."

Buttons flew in all directions as he tore his shirt off, struggled out of his breeches, boots, and stockings. Almost crying with need, he crawled up her body, nudging her legs apart as he went.

Her visible passion, so clearly displayed by her flushed cheeks, hitched breath, and darkened eyes drove him further to the edge. She was everything he ever needed. He would move mountains to keep her by his side. Despite his feelings of inadequacy in keeping her safe, he had grown to love this woman with his entire being. Whatever it took, he would one day hear her profess her love.

His fingers assuring himself she was ready for him, he plunged into her depths, shuddering as her liquid heat surrounded him. Knowing he wasn't going to last very long, he shifted his body to rub his thumb over her swollen nub. Blood pounded in his ears, hearing no sounds, seeing only her.

Nothing was as beautiful as Abigail in the throes of passion. Her lips were plump with his kisses, her head thrashed back and forth, cries of release coming from deep inside her. Within minutes he felt her explosion, her muscles contracting around him, milking him, taking everything he had to give. There was nothing left between them to hide.

Giving one final thrust, he collapsed on top of her, their limbs a tangled mess. His lungs burned, dew covered both of their bodies, and his life would never again be the same.

Chapter Thirteen

Drake yanked on Abaccus's reins, leaning forward to keep his seat as the horse's front legs rose in the air. Within seconds Joseph joined him as he reined in the same shiny black stallion from the other morning. Both men sat in silence as they caught their breath at the end of their early morning gallop along Rotten Row.

With the sun only partially over the horizon, a hazy mist blanketed the area, dew drops clinging to leaves and grass. Air not yet spoiled by the summer heat, which would soon release the stench from the river and other pungent spots, encouraged them to inhale deeply.

Soon the Season would end, and driven by the heat and stink of the city, most of the *ton* would retire to their summer estates until Parliament was in session once again. During that time, house parties, holiday balls, and autumn fox hunting would keep the Quality entertained.

Joseph pushed the thought to the back of his mind that

had Abigail not married him, she would soon be ensconced in the safety of Manchester Manor, instead of dodging bullets and stamping out fires in Addysby End.

Still in a deep sleep after another rousing session with his wife the night before, Joseph had received a summons from his brother-in-law's footman to meet him at the stables for an early morning ride. With Abigail slumbering peacefully, he'd arisen, quickly dressed, and joined Drake. No words, besides a nod and a brief "good morning," had yet to pass between the men.

In the past three days while Joseph and Abigail had visited Manchester House, no opportunity had arisen for them to have a private conversation. Penelope kept them busy with picnics, walks in the park, a musicale at the home of Lord and Lady Beckham, and of course, fawning over the new heir. As peaceful as this interlude had been, he desperately needed to gain Drake's perspective on his dilemma.

"I don't suppose you would consider leaving Abigail here with me?" Drake said, staring out at the expanse of trees and grass in Hyde Park.

"I would place her in a high-walled convent if I thought she would go along with it."

Drake chuckled and shook his head. "I tried threatening that when she turned down suitor after suitor. I doubt you would have any more luck than I did."

"However, I'm torn between letting her know how very concerned I am for her welfare, or, allowing her to believe these occasions were truly accidents." Joseph shifted in his saddle and turned to Drake. "What would you do if this were Penelope?"

All the blood left Manchester's face.

"Exactly," Joseph said with a tight smile. "If I could think of a good reason for her to remain here with you, I would try it. But your sister tends to be a bit on the stubborn side."

"Really? I hadn't noticed."

"So what are your suggestions? I admit I am at a loss. I've been running names around in my head for days, but can't think of anyone who would have cause to harm her."

"Oftentimes it comes down to money. Greed."

Joseph paused for a moment. "There is no one who would benefit from Abigail's death."

"No. You already own everything she had when you married."

He stiffened as a flash of anger shot through him. "Don't even suggest such a thing."

"I wasn't. I was merely ruminating. I would never think that you would hurt her. It's obvious you care very deeply for my sister. And she for you." His eyes twinkled as he regarded him. "Curious, that. It certainly hasn't taken very much time."

Joseph's heart thumped at Drake's casual words. *Abigail cared for him?* Not likely. Despite an enthusiastic bed partner, and an accommodating and caring wife, she seemed to want to stick to her word to not offer him more. She'd been hurt once before, and would not open up her heart again.

"I will hire a man to investigate these accidents," Drake said.

"There is no need. If what I've told you has convinced you an investigation is in order, I can do that myself."

Drake shook head. "Anyone you hire from Addysby

End would be known and would find it difficult to question the townspeople. I can send a man from here, who will slip into village life as someone leaving behind the burden of Town for a short holiday."

"Then you agree this warrants action?"

"I trust you too much to discount your concerns. I know you for a man who doesn't imagine monsters where there are none." Drake used his thighs to spur Abaccus forward. "My man will be settled in Addysby End before you return home."

Joseph followed behind, relieved that something useful was being done.

• • •

The day after they arrived home, Abigail, Joseph, and Lady Durham gathered around a large table in the new school building that was piled high with books, slates, and chalk. They'd just finished unpacking supplies for the students. The building was completed, and within days they would begin visiting the families who had young children, to convince the parents to send their offspring for lessons on a regular basis.

"How was your visit to London?" Lady Durham directed her attention to Abigail.

"Quite nice. It was lovely to visit with my brother and his family. Their son is growing rapidly."

"They tend to do that." She smiled warmly. "I assume you are recovered from the dreadful fire?"

Abigail started and frowned. "Yes. How did you know about it?"

Lady Durham waved her hand. "Oh, I stopped by to

visit with you while you were in London, and Manning mentioned it."

Abigail and Joseph shared a quick glance. She didn't want to call Lady Durham a liar, but Manning was not a house servant who enjoyed gossip. Perhaps one of the lower servants had blabbed and Lady Durham was trying to protect her. In any event, Abigail would have a conversation with the staff about the need to protect the privacy of their employers.

Joseph brushed the dust from the boxes off his jacket. "Yes. My wife has recovered, and I believe the visit to her family helped restore her spirits. It is very nice of you to inquire after her well-being. Now I suggest we distribute the supplies among the tables so we will be ready to receive our students."

Lady Durham jumped as if booted from behind. "Of course."

All three gathered up Bibles, primers, slates, and chalk and placed them on the tables.

"Do you find you miss the excitement of London, Lady Abigail?" Lady Durham smiled serenely as she placed items on the tables.

"Not particularly. I think I had my fill of that type of excitement over the past few years."

"It is just too bad a lovely woman such as yourself is stuck in this little village."

Abigail cast a glance at Joseph, but it didn't seem he paid attention. "Not at all. I enjoy the town and the villagers."

"Yes, we are a wonderful little group, are we not? A bit provincial, perhaps."

What precisely was Lady Durham trying to say? Had

Abigail given her, or any of the other townspeople, the idea that she was not happy here? Hopefully, that was not the case because she really wanted to be accepted by Joseph's congregation, and not viewed as some high stepping Londoner who was bored with anything not associated with Town.

Lady Durham wandered in Joseph's direction, and began a conversation with him, leaving Abigail with her thoughts.

Thoughts that soon turned to a place she should probably not visit. Heat rose to her face when she remembered dropping to her knees in front of Joseph and using her mouth in such a shocking way. She'd smiled at his jolt, and then the way he'd grasped her head, almost pulling her hair out.

It was too bad she hadn't thought to grab that wicked book of Drake's before they'd left Manchester House. What other scandalous things could she do to shock her husband? An image from the book flashed in her mind, recalling Joseph's remarks about tying her to the bed for reasons other than keeping her there after her injury. Could that be what he'd been referring to? Oh dear. That did sound interesting. A giggle escaped, but Joseph and Lady Durham were deep in conversation and didn't notice her.

Then, as if a cloud passed over on a sunny day, the words she'd spoken to Joseph about banning him from her bed once she learned she was with child leapt to the front of her mind. Why had she done something so foolish?

Most likely in her naivety, she'd not counted on enjoying his "attentions" so much. Well, when the time came, she would have to make it appear as if Joseph had persuaded her to change her mind. As long as she continued to hold her heart from him, life would be pleasant.

Though, did she want more than *pleasant?*

. . .

A slight knock on his office door dragged Joseph's attention from the latest report sent by his Cornwall estate steward. As soon as the school was running smoothly, he and Abigail would make a trip there. Once again, he would have to engage the services of the young curate from his father's church to tend to matters here. "Yes?"

Manning entered the room, holding a small card in his hand. "Sir, an individual has called and wishes to speak with you."

Joseph noted the absence of the word "gentleman" in Manning's announcement. It amazed him how servants seemed very aware of class distinctions. He glanced at the card:

Mr. Melvin Grundell, London, England.

A name unknown to him. "Send him in."

Mr. Grundell was as nondescript as a person can be. He was of medium height and weight. His light brown hair covered what would soon be a bald spot at the front of his head. He wore spectacles on a rather ordinary nose. His eyes could have been anywhere between brown and hazel. His neck cloth hung limp over his brown jacket. In all, he could spend an hour in a crowd and never be remarked upon.

Joseph waved to the chair in front of his desk. "How may I assist you, Mr. Grundell?"

The man sat on the edge of the chair, leaning forward. "I am here to assist *you,* sir. The Duke of Manchester has engaged me to investigate the accidents your wife appears to have suffered of late."

Joseph tapped his pen on the desk. "Yes. He did say he would be sending you. I am most grateful for any light you can shed on this matter."

Mr. Grundell reached into his pocket, withdrew a small notebook and flipped open the pages. "Now start from the beginning, Mr. Fox, and tell me everything that has happened to your lovely wife since she arrived." He looked up. "How long ago was that?"

"A little more than two months."

Once again, reliving what Abigail had suffered in such a short period of time angered and frightened him. Mr. Grundell took notes, every once in a while looking up at Joseph, but never interrupting. Laid out the way it was, he wondered if the man believed him to be a case for Bedlam. Why else would he imagine that someone was purposely attempting to harm a woman who had no connection to the village prior to their marriage?

"Now, Mr. Fox. Can you think of anyone who has a reason to dislike your new wife? Who might have a reason to wish you hadn't married her?"

Joseph leaned back and rested his elbow on the arm of his chair, his thumb and index finger bracing his chin. "I don't understand."

Mr. Grundell checked his notes. "It seems to me everything was real peaceful and quiet-like until you arrived back here with a bride."

"I doubt my marriage has anything to do with this."

"Ah, it could, if there is someone who feels like he or she lost something when you married. Had you made promises to another lady?"

"Of course not! I would never dishonor a woman in that way."

Mr. Grundell raised his palm. "I meant no insult, sir. I'm wondering if perhaps someone is not merely unhappy with your wife, but with the fact that she *is* your wife."

An image of Lady Durham flashed before him, but he quickly dismissed it. The widow was a well-bred lady whom he had befriended when she'd arrived in Addysby End. She was still in mourning for her husband. *No,* he assured himself. What Mr. Grundell was suggesting could not have anything to do with this situation. "Do you suppose Lady Abigail may have an enemy who followed her here from London?"

"When I spoke with His Grace, he mentioned something about his sister being jilted before she married you."

He nodded. "She was. She'd been betrothed to Viscount Redgrave, and the cad ran out on her."

Mr. Grundell jotted that information down, then flipped his notebook closed. "I have taken up residence at the Addysby Inn. As far as the villagers know, I am merely here on holiday, at my doctor's advice." He rose and shoved the notebook into his pocket. "I would like you to make a list of anyone who has access to your property. Employees, friends, neighbors. Once you have compiled the listing, bring it with you to your service on Sunday. I will get it from you then."

"Very well. I should also tell you I don't wish my wife to be upset by this investigation. She is not to know about it at all."

"Do you think that's wise?"

"She believes these are accidents. I prefer not to worry

her by suggesting that perhaps someone wishes her ill. However, I have arranged with members of my staff to make certain she is not alone when I cannot be with her."

"Very well, Mr. Fox. I will do my best to keep my queries from her."

"Thank you." Joseph opened the library door. "Manning will see you out. Good day."

Joseph turned and wandered to the window. Abigail strolled in the garden, bending occasionally to examine a flower up closer. Ten steps behind her, one of the footmen followed.

The sun glinted off the gold and emerald band on her finger as she reached to pick one of the gardener's prized roses, then sniffed it, closing her eyes. His heart gave a tug as he watched her innocently enjoying a walk in the garden. Yet, as he'd discovered the day of the fire, she was not even safe here in her own home. He hated to think one of his staff was behind these accidents. He shook his head in denial. They had all been with him since he'd arrived several years ago.

He rubbed the back of his neck, then sighed and returned to his desk. Life could be very enjoyable once the mystery of her accidents was solved. Then he could spend time convincing Abigail that love could be a part of their marriage.

In fact, maybe he would not wait until then before he wooed her. They'd had no real courtship, when most young couples discover each other and fall in love. Most likely, all of Abigail's memories of them being children together were helping to keep her more mature emotions in check.

A courtship was a fine idea. He would take her on a

picnic soon. They would laze about on a blanket and share food and a bottle of wine. He'd encourage her to remove her stockings and shoes and wade in the creek. If they found a secluded enough place, maybe he would make love to her. Right there in the open before God and all the small animals.

Winning her love could be very enjoyable, indeed. Something that was very important to him.

That, and discovering who was trying to kill her.

Chapter Fourteen

Lady Edith Durham accepted the driver's hand and stepped up to enter her coach. She wiggled a bit to settle in, smoothing her skirts as the carriage jerked, and then eased into a steady ride toward the village. She clenched her fists and stared out the window. Lady Abigail had to be the luckiest person in all of England. Who would have thought getting rid of one bothersome woman would be so difficult? If she didn't oust *Mrs. Fox* from her snug position alongside Joseph, Edith would be stuck in this miserable village for the rest of her life, with no more than a couple hundred pounds each year doled out by the stingy Lord Durham.

Curse the earl and his insipid wife, who'd looked down her long nose, and pulled her skirts close when they'd been introduced. As if Edith was something nasty on her shoe. Well, she would show them. She'd show the entire world. Once Lady Abigail was out of the picture, no one would stand between her and Joseph's money. No one.

A few hours later, her errands completed, she bid the innocuous shopkeeper good day and waved at her useless driver to move the coach forward to where she waited. Honestly, if stupid were a hanging offense, the man would be rotting in the ground. Once he arrived, she had to stand tapping her foot as he lumbered down from his perch and ambled over to open the door. She scowled as she swept past him, comforting herself with visions of the look on his face when she told him his services were no longer needed, and he would receive no reference.

Ensconced in the carriage, she leaned back and gazed out at the passing scenery. Languidly fanning herself, she noticed a man and a woman off in the distance, apparently enjoying a summer afternoon picnic. As she watched, they stood, and strolled to the creek hand-in-hand.

Young lovers. At one time she would have envied them. Now, after years of conniving and scratching out a living by any means she could, love was not something she cared about. Money was all that mattered. Money to buy all the gowns, slippers, and fancy coaches she wanted. And jewels. She would have diamonds and emeralds. There were times when she felt way beyond her four and twenty years.

She continued to view the man and woman as they splashed each other with water from the creek. The woman laughed, gathered her skirts in her fist, and they both stepped farther into the water. Edith continued to study them. The man pulled the woman to his side, wrapping his arms around her. She released her skirts to slide her hands up his chest, the heavy material dragging in the water, although she didn't seem to notice — or care. He nuzzled her neck, then took her mouth in a searing kiss.

Any uneasiness she might have felt watching such a private scene was quickly pushed away. If they wished to make a spectacle of themselves in pubic, far be it from her to care. She had more important things to concern herself with. She sat back as the noise of her carriage must have caught the man's attention, and he broke the kiss and turned toward the road.

Joseph!

Anger raced through her like a galloping steed. Pounding her fist on her leg, she whipped the curtain closed and cursed the cozy sight. This could not continue.

She thumped on the carriage ceiling. "Hurry up, you dolt. I would like to get home sometime today."

There must be some sort of mischief she could cause them. It was time to put an end to this botheration.

• • •

Abigail had been thrilled when Joseph stopped in before luncheon and suggested they take the afternoon off and have Cook pack a picnic basket for them. He assured her his sermon for Sunday was finished, and his only student for the day had happily departed for home. "It is too lovely a day for us not to enjoy it."

More than pleased to put away the lessons she'd been working on for the opening of the school next week, Abigail hurried to the kitchen. Cook had quickly put together a basket with cheese, fruit, bread, and cold meat. Joseph joined her in the kitchen, and giving her a wink, slid a bottle of wine into the basket.

Now the remnants of their feast littered the blanket

Joseph had spread out for them, and they were enjoying the last of the wine. "My mother is fond of picnics. I'm sure you remember, since you practically lived at our house when we were growing up."

"Yes, I remember it well. The dignity of your mother's station in life never kept her from having fun. Her escapades were well known in Donridge Heath." He extended his hand toward her. "Come. Let's enjoy the coolness of the creek again."

They'd been in and out of the refreshing water all afternoon. They spent some time playing in the water, splashing each other. Already barefoot, Abigail gathered her skirts in her hand and sighed with pleasure as the cooling liquid swirled between her toes. Joseph wrapped his arms around her from behind, nuzzling her neck. She tilted her head, her lips coming within an inch of his, then dropped her skirts as she encircled his neck. Something flashed in Joseph's eyes that started her senses humming. He dipped his head that mere inch and took her mouth in a sizzling kiss. He nibbled on her lower lip, then urged her mouth open.

She ran her palms over his sun-warmed muscled back, the hardness of his body against hers making her weak. The scent of him, so familiar to her now, set her blood to pumping, and her lower parts to weeping. His hands moved up her arms and gripped her head, moving it one way, and then the other, deepening their kiss until Abigail was flush with passion.

• • •

Joseph broke from the kiss and looked up at a carriage

rumbling by on the road. A reminder that the spot he'd chosen for their picnic did not have the privacy for this sort of behavior. *Oh, how I'd like to lay her down on the soft, warm grass and have my way with her. Watch her eyes darken with passion, her breath come in pants, her naked breasts rise and fall. . .*

Instead he kissed her hand, and brushed the errant curls from her cheek. "Perhaps we should pack up." Then he could get her home and finish what he had started.

At first somewhat dazed, Abigail nodded, and hands joined, they strolled back to the blanket where she sat and rolled on her stockings. He tried his best to avoid watching her perform such a provocative activity. Sweat beaded his forehead as she bent her knee, causing her skirt to slide down to the tops of her long legs, leaving all that creamy skin exposed. She glanced at him with an enticing smile, and he knew her thoughts were moving in the same direction as his.

He hurried to pack up the food, then slipped on his own stockings and shoes. Abigail folded the blanket, and with everything set to right, they headed to the waiting carriage. They grinned at each other when Joseph had to wake the driver from an afternoon slumber. Once they were settled, and he'd signaled they were ready, he turned his attention to Abigail. "There is an assembly dance next week."

Her face lit up, causing a twinge of guilt to nudge at him. Perhaps she did miss London and all the balls and entertainments.

"How nice. I haven't been to a dance since I left London." She paused and tilted her head, bringing his attention to her full lips. Berry red lips still swollen from his kiss. "It will be quite pleasant to dance again."

He reached for her hand. "Do you miss London? Shall we make another trip there for the end of the Season?"

She shook her head. "No. I am truly not sorry to have left all of that behind. I find I prefer our village life. And we have the school to think of."

The pad of his thumb rubbed tiny circles on the sensitive flesh on the inside of her wrist. She licked her lips, making him wish the carriage would speed up.

"I am looking forward to holding you in my arms as we waltz around the room."

"Is the waltz allowed? When I was a girl attending assembly dances in Donridge Heath the waltz had not yet been introduced. And it was a good thing since the matrons were very strict about the rules."

The memories of trying so hard to ignore Abigail at those gatherings flooded back. She had been lovely even as a young miss, and it had saddened him to see the hurt in her eyes when he'd brushed off her unsophisticated attempts to garner his attention. In addition to the unwritten rule of avoiding one's best friend's sister, the difference in their stations had necessitated his actions. Never would he have guessed she would end up his wife. Life certainly took one down paths never imagined.

"We are quite sophisticated here, you know."

Her eyebrows rose. "Then I look forward to it even more."

Pulling her onto his lap, he licked the outside of her ear and murmured, "Not as much as I look forward to our arrival home." If the coach didn't hurry, he would scandalize his wife by taking her right here in a moving carriage.

Although, based on her past actions, perhaps she would not be so scandalized, after all.

. . .

Like all country assemblies, the young women of Addysby End had spared no effort in presenting their best visage. Hair was arranged in artful displays of curls, beads, and feathers. Some older gowns had been refreshed by added ribbons and ruffles. Many of the young girls from more prosperous families were attired in new gowns of the latest fashions and colors. Gentlemen wore their evening clothes with style and sophistication. The only difference between the assembly and a London ballroom was the lack of pretense.

Here, it was obvious everyone had come for a good time. In London, it was all about seeing and being seen, or a fear that if one did not attend a function it would be assumed one had not been invited. Which allowed for much gossip in the days that followed.

Abigail's heart lightened at the lovely decorations the ladies of the town had provided. A table along the wall held a punch bowl and plates with thin slices of cake. A group of musicians had gathered in one corner, tuning up instruments. The buzz and laughter as more people arrived gave the room a sense of holiday.

They'd barely made their way across the room, stopping to greet various guests when Lady Durham approached them, her hands outstretched. "My dears, it is so good to see you. It has been ages." In the way of the *ton*, she took Abigail's hands and air-kissed her cheek.

She beamed at Joseph as he took her hand and kissed it. "My lady, it is a pleasure, as always."

"Isn't it exciting to have such a turnout in our little village?" She turned to Abigail. "I am sure this is nothing like you are used to. After several Seasons in London, you no doubt view our meager efforts as pitiful. How many Seasons was it you remained unmarried?"

Abigail bit her lip to keep from laughing, amused that the woman seemed to feel sorry for her. Had Abigail kept count of all the gentlemen whom she'd turned down over the past few years, they could fill half the assembly room. "Three, actually."

Lady Durham patted her hand. "Well, I'm sure it was quite a relief when Mr. Fox rescued you from all of that."

Joseph cleared his throat as Abigail's eyebrows rose. Before she could respond, he turned to her. "Sweetheart, would you honor me with a dance?"

"Oh, how quaint. Husband and wife dancing together." Lady Durham tittered and waved her hand toward the dance floor as they both regarded her. "Have a good time. I shall circulate for a while."

"That was strange," Abigail said as she settled her hand on Joseph's shoulder.

"She means well. I'm sure she doesn't realize how her words sound to others."

"Most likely." They parted as the dance began, and continued to move smoothly through the steps.

• • •

Edith reined in her anger as she circulated through the

ballroom, nodding and smiling. Every time she saw the looks that passed between Joseph and Lady Abigail, it took all of her self-control to not screech like a fishwife and stomp her foot. Not the impression she'd striven for since she'd left the hell-hole of her previous life behind.

Her attention was taken by a tall gentleman entering the assembly room. A very interesting man with a certain air about him. Someone she had never seen before. Not one to be considered handsome, nevertheless, the way he wore his clothes and carried himself attracted her. His manner spoke of power and money. An older woman clung to his arm as they slowly made their way along the line of those who had forfeited the dance floor in lieu of conversation.

Without seeming to rush, Edith wended her way through the crowd, her eyes never leaving her prey. The gentleman seemed affable, conversing with anyone who approached him. The elderly woman's eyes flashed, taking in all around her, as if she hadn't been out in society for quite some time.

Edith neared the couple and curtsied. "Good evening. I am Lady Durham, and may I wish you welcome to our little gathering."

The gentleman took her hand and kissed it. "My lady, it is a pleasure. Viscount Sterling at your service, and may I present my great-aunt, Lady Blunden?"

"My lady," Edith curtsied once more. "I hope you are enjoying yourself."

"It has been years, my dear, since I have attended one of these events. I found it necessary to drag my nephew from London to attend me. Now isn't that a terrible predicament to be in, I ask you?"

Edith turned to the viscount. "You are recently down

from London?"

"Yes. I plan to stay a few weeks."

"And is Lady Sterling with you?"

"She is. My darling wife is just now recovering from a chill, and decided to stay at home this evening."

Well, that answered that question. Unless he was interested in taking a mistress, Lord Sterling would serve her no purpose. The reference to his wife as his darling didn't bode well for the likelihood of any sort of dalliance. She sighed inwardly, once more frustrated at the lack of potential candidates for her benefit in this backward place.

"I say, is that Lady Abigail?" The viscount raised his looking glass to his eye. "Indeed it is. I wondered to where she'd disappeared."

"You know Lady Abigail?"

"Indeed, I do. All of London was familiar with her recent problem." He lowered his glass and shook his head. "A terrible time for the girl, I imagine. I wonder why she is here."

Edith's heart began to pound. *Her recent problem? Terrible time? How very intriguing. The perfect Lady Abigail with a problem that made her disappear from London? Do tell.*

How could she get Sterling to elaborate on the subject without seeming overly inquisitive?

"I apologize for keeping you standing, my lady," Edith said eying the older woman with solicitude. "May I lead you to a chair, and obtain some refreshment for you?"

"That would be lovely, my dear." The woman smiled and accepted her nephew's arm as they followed Edith to the line of chairs against the wall.

Her head spun with possibilities. What sort of a problem could Lady Abigail have gotten herself into? That could very well explain her sudden appearance as Joseph's wife.

In all the time she'd known Joseph, he had never mentioned Lady Abigail. In fact, he'd never shown favor to any woman, other than friendship. It would be interesting to know if Joseph was privy to *her problem*. Inwardly, she giggled with glee.

While the ladies chatted, Sterling retrieved glasses of punch and slices of cake for them. Once he returned and settled alongside his aunt, Edith set her cup and plate aside and leaned closer to the couple. "We were so glad to see Lady Abigail so nicely settled here in our little village."

"Yes. Again I must say I am surprised to see her. There were many in London who wondered where she'd gone."

"It was such a difficult time for her." Edith shook her head, desperately hoping Sterling would say more without her having to ask.

"Well, be assured that despite the nasty gossip surrounding her, Lady Sterling and I placed the blame for the catastrophe right on Redgrave's doorstep."

Redgrave?

"I must agree. The man is a cad." Edith quelled the desire to grab him by his fancy neck cloth and shake the story out of him. This was getting good. Had the girl been compromised and Redgrave refused to do the honorable thing? Had she left London labeled a trollop? Her heart did a lively *pirouette*.

"What happened, Sterling?" The older lady asked.

At last! Edith could have bent over and kissed the woman's powdered cheek.

"It was most unfortunate, Aunt. Lady Abigail is the Duke of Manchester's sister. She was betrothed to Lord Redgrave, and a few weeks before the wedding, he ran off with another woman." He shook his head. "Disgraceful."

"Oh, my. The poor girl." Lady Blunden sniffed.

Sterling turned toward Edith. "Why is she here in Addysby End?"

"Lady Abigail is married to Mr. Joseph Fox, the rector at St. Gertrude's Church here in the village."

Lord Sterling leaned back in his chair, a slight smile on his face. "I am happy to hear that. I must make a point to speak with her, and wish her and her husband well. She is a lovely girl from an outstanding family."

"Oh, yes," Edith said. "We all absolutely *love* her."

Chapter Fifteen

Two days after the assembly, Abigail headed to the stables for an early morning ride. Joseph was busy with one of his students, so the younger footman, David, accompanied her. She suspected Joseph insisted on her having company everywhere she went because of his concerns about her accidents.

She'd given the situation a lot of thought, herself. Perhaps these accidents were not truly "accidents." Joseph had seemed to hint at that, but she'd dismissed it. Everyone she'd met so far in this lovely little village had been welcoming and pleasant. Maybe it was time for her to do some investigating of her own. Not that she had cause to suspect anyone, but she should certainly begin looking at everyone a bit differently.

Despite the fear she lived with each day, she would not hide herself or cower in her room. If someone did intend to harm her, she would find out whom, and turn him over to the authorities. How she would accomplish that feat remained to be seen, but just having that resolve boosted her spirits. In any event, after three days of rain, she intended to take advantage of the sun and enjoy her ride.

Soon she and Joseph would take an entire day visiting with the villagers and signing up students for school. She was very excited about the project. She'd spent hours designing lesson plans for different age students, drawing on her exercises from her governess.

She and her sisters had studied French, watercolors, music, and embroidering–things a gentlewoman would need to know. That, of course, would be of no benefit to her students. But they had also been schooled in reading, arithmetic, and writing. Those skills would be of great importance to the village children and help them obtain a better life for themselves.

The stable master assisted her onto her horse, Samara. The mare had been her twelfth year birthday present. She still remembered her excitement when Father had paraded the beautiful Palomino out of the stables and right up to her. He'd handed her the reins and had said, "Happy birthday, sweetheart. A beautiful animal for a beautiful young lady."

Even now tears rimmed her eyes at the memory. Although her father had been gone for a few years, there were days her heart ached with missing him. He'd been right there in the midst of their loud and loving family, big as life, and then a throw from his horse, breaking his neck, had taken him away.

Before the reminder had her dissolving into tears, she took off, the mud spewing forth from the horse's hoofs as she rounded the corner and headed in the opposite direction of town. The air was warm and clear—unlike her carriage rides in Hyde Park during the fashionable hour. Another thing that she certainly didn't miss. Not only were the visitors there to merely see and be seen, by late afternoon in the summertime, the air would be stifling and odorous.

Once she and David left behind the cottages that dotted the countryside, Abigail gave her horse her head, enjoying the wind ripping through her hair which had come loose from her topknot. Her heart beat faster as the horse sped along. Up ahead, a low hedge loomed, and she aimed straight for it.

Samara had always been a wonderful jumper, and it had been a while since they'd been out together to enjoy the exhilaration of flying over an obstacle—for a few seconds soaring in the air. Grinning, she spurred the animal faster, leaning low over her back as they approached the hedge.

Samara's front legs left the ground just as Abigail heard a snap, and felt the saddle slide off the horse. She kicked her foot free of the stirrup, and threw her hands up as the ground seemed to come rushing up to her.

I'm going to die. Just like Papa.

• • •

"Sir, Mr. Melvin Grundell to see you," Manning announced in his usual stiff tone.

As Grundell entered the room, Joseph was once again surprised at how little he remembered of the man. Truly a nondescript individual, which was probably a major asset in his line of work. He put his hand out to shake before they both settled into their chairs.

"I've come to give you my weekly report, Mr. Fox."

Joseph nodded to proceed and the man continued. "I've made some inquiries into the very short list of individuals you gave me who have access to the property. So far no one falls under the category of suspicious."

"That is good to hear. I hate to think that someone I trust, who has entry to my property, would try to harm Lady Abigail."

"There are still one or two from your list I have not had the opportunity to speak with yet. And another individual whose background I'm investigating. But until I have any solid answers for you, I prefer to wait until all my information has been received."

Joseph would break into a cold sweat whenever he imagined the devastation he would feel if anything happened to Abigail. Their friendship marriage had turned into so much more. At least where he was concerned. Abigail was everything he could ever want in a wife. Smart, funny, beautiful, and an active bed partner. She would be a wonderful mother, and life for them could be very good.

He marveled at how fortunate he'd been to stop in to visit Manchester that day he was in London looking for patrons for his school. To think if he'd not been there right at that moment, his life would be so very different.

Although he had had an interest in Manchester's wife, Penelope, back when Drake was still unconvinced that he loved the woman, no one else had ever attracted him since. Lady Durham had seemed to cast some intriguing looks in his direction. She was a pleasant woman, but something about her had held him back from any serious consideration as his wife.

Mr. Grundall flipped his notebook closed. "That is about

all I have to report at this time. I assume that everything has been quiet since the fire?"

"Yes. I have either myself or a footman with Lady Abigail at all times."

The investigator nodded. "That is a very good idea, Mr. Fox. Don't you worry, we'll run this person to the ground."

The men shook hands and Grundell took his leave. Joseph stretched and headed to the front door where Manning kept watch. "Is Lady Abigail about?"

"She left with David about a half an hour ago for a ride."

Joseph wandered to the library where his student was busy conjugating Latin verbs. He checked over his work and returned to his office. He sat behind the desk, and leaned back, propping his feet on the edge.

Within minutes, the front door of the house burst open, and shouting brought him to his feet. He pushed his chair back so rapidly it fell over. Ignoring it, he strode to the door and stepped into the corridor to see David carrying Abigail in his arms.

All the blood left his head and his heart began to pound. "What happened?" He raced forward and took his wife from the footman's arms, shifting her so she rested against his chest.

"My lady was thrown from her horse when she attempted to jump a hedge." The young man was sweating and had a wild look in his eyes.

Joseph started up the stairs. "Manning, send for the doctor." At this rate, he should probably offer the doctor a room in his home.

"Yes, sir."

He hugged Abigail's body close to his, inhaling her

sweet scent. There were slight scratches on her forehead and face, and as he studied her, her eyes flicked open. "Joseph?"

"Thank God." He buried his face in her neck and fought back tears.

• • •

Lady Durham had been considering how she could use the information she'd garnered from Lord Sterling at the assembly. Lady Abigail had been practically left at the altar. How amusing. She scowled. And then like a knight in shining armor, Joseph had swooped in and rescued her from her shame. Why were the women born to privilege never left to suffer for long? There was always someone to extricate them from any type of hardship.

She sipped on her gin, wrinkling her nose at the lower class drink. Closing her eyes, she imagined this Lord Redgrave entering the scene and causing Joseph to send Abigail back to her family. Then she could offer herself as his mistress, which could pay quite well.

"Stupid!" She slammed the glass down. The man was a rector, for God's sake. He'd never take a mistress. The only way she would get her hands on his money was as his wife. Which meant the lovely, jilted, Lady Abigail had to die. Perhaps after Edith's little tinkering with dear little Mrs. Fox's saddle, the woman was already dead.

She snorted. Not likely. Lady Abigail indeed had a guardian angel. The next attempt had to be the last time. But meanwhile she would wreak a little havoc with their cozy relationship. Maybe Joseph wouldn't guard her so carefully if he thought his wife's heart was with another.

Throwing back the last of the clear liquid in her glass, she broke into a grin. Yes, indeed. A little suspicion between husband and wife was a good thing. She swung her bare feet off the table top and hurried to the bedroom to change into her "lady" clothes.

· · ·

It was late afternoon when Lady Abigail put her embroidering aside as her visitor entered the drawing room. "Lady Durham, how nice of you to call."

Abigail had recovered from her fall, only having bruised herself. The thick bushes she'd landed in, plus her years as an avid horsewoman had saved her, since she'd known enough to kick her foot free of the stirrups before she'd flown off Samara.

Despite her assurances to Joseph that she was fine, merely sore in a few places, he had insisted on sending for the doctor who pronounced her fit, and after a day of bed rest, able to resume her normal activities.

She'd spent the time in bed composing a list of anyone she suspected might wish to cause her harm. It was a very short list. In fact, the only person on the list—her current guest—she had scratched off, feeling abashed at even thinking the woman would attempt to harm her.

If anything, she felt sorry for Lady Durham. There was something about her that seemed to not fit. Almost as if she didn't belong in the world she found herself. And to be such a young, attractive widow in this small village.

"I have just rung for tea. I hope you will join me."

Lady Durham settled in and removed her gloves. "I

would love to."

"Sweetheart, have you seen. . ." Joseph stopped as he strode through the doorway, papers clutched in his hand, and noted Abigail's guest. "I apologize, I didn't realize you had company."

Something flashed in Edith's eyes that had Abigail inhaling sharply. But before she could even analyze it, the look was gone. Almost as if Abigail had imagined it. Dismissing her fancifulness, she smiled. "Lady Durham was good enough to stop by to visit."

"My lady," Joseph said, bowing. "It is a pleasure to see you."

"I am surprised to see you, Mr. Fox. I thought you were busy with the Bible study class on Wednesday afternoons."

"Right you are, my lady. I was about to set off, horribly late, I'm afraid." He turned to Abigail. "Have you seen my notes for this week's sermon?"

Abigail smiled at Joseph's forgetfulness. Although, with all he had on his mind, and now her safety added to his burden, it was no wonder he kept misplacing things. "Yes. You left them on the desk in my sitting room. I put them on the shelf behind your desk in the study."

"Thank you, my dear." He turned to Lady Durham. "I can't imagine what I would do without her."

Abigail leaned her head to one side as Joseph kissed her quickly on the cheek. "I will see you at dinner."

In a whirlwind he was gone, leaving the women in peaceful silence. "He is most energetic," Abigail said.

"Very much so."

The footman entered with the tea tray, and Abigail busied herself with pouring tea and passing the tray of soft cheese and cucumber sandwiches, and lemon tarts to her guest.

I can't imagine what I would do without her

Abigail warmed at Joseph's words as Lady Durham began a lengthy discourse on one of the villager's recent troubles with her husband. Listening with half an ear, Abigail's thoughts wandered to how Joseph had held her so tightly, as he'd climbed the stairs to their bedchamber the day she had been thrown from Samara.

She'd been only too happy to drape her arms around his neck and breathe in his scent. Warm, spicy, and male. Familiar and comfortable. He'd placed her with extreme gentleness onto the bed and had sat alongside her, stroking her cheek with his fingertips, murmuring soft words.

"I want to wrap you in my arms, and never let you go," he'd said, his voice thick with emotion.

At one time she would have assumed the saddle hadn't been tightened correctly, but after a few well-placed questions to the stable master, she'd learned the girth strap had been cut. Not all the way through, just enough to weaken it as she rode. Another "accident" that obviously was an attempt to hurt her.

Now her fright had turned to anger. She'd done nothing to justify such treatment. If someone was attempting to scare her away from Addysby End, they'd chosen the wrong person to bully. She was here, and this is where she would stay.

Joseph seemed to watch her with such vigilance it was almost comical. Although, truth be known, the only time she felt completely safe and secure was in their bed when he held her in his arms. But they could not spend their days and nights snuggled under the covers. Soon she would have to make a visit into town to see if she could uncover anything that might be of interest to her investigation.

If only Joseph would share his concerns with her. They could put their heads together to solve this mystery. But with the protectiveness he surrounded her with, any suggestion from her that they work together to solve this would most likely end in him sending her to her brother.

"My dear, if you would excuse me, I need to use the facilities."

Lady Durham's request broke into Abigail's thoughts, reminding her she was entertaining a guest and should not allow her mind to wander.

"Of course. Let me ring for someone to accompany you."

"No need for that. I can find them by myself. If you will excuse me?"

Before Abigail could insist on being a good hostess, Lady Durham had exited the room, leaving her once more with her thoughts.

• • •

Edith hurried from the drawing room before Abigail changed her mind and sent for a maid to follow her about. Her heart pounding, she headed directly to Joseph's study. Although sure he had already left for his Bible class, nevertheless, she tapped gently on the closed door. No answer.

She slipped into the room after glancing up and down the corridor to assure herself no one lurked about to see her. This time of the day the servants were finished with their morning work, and should be preparing for the evening's activities.

Withdrawing a torn piece of vellum from under her bodice, she smiled and dropped the missive onto the floor, and with her shoe, pushed it almost underneath the settee. She moved back and tilted her head, studying the note. It had to look as though someone had dropped it accidentally. Using her toe, she shifted it a bit, then walked back to the door and turned, studying the room. Yes. When Joseph entered the room, the piece of paper would catch his eye. Now she only hoped that Abigail didn't make a habit of popping into his study. Because the next time Joseph opened this door, he would find her little note.

If only she could be here to see his face. Adjusting her gown, she smoothed back her hair and raised her chin. *Let's see how much of a sweetheart Lady Abigail is once Joseph sees the letter.*

Satisfied with her afternoon's work, she checked the corridor, then stealthily closed the study door and returned to the drawing room.

· · ·

The next morning Joseph and Abigail parted after breakfast, agreeing to meet in an hour to call on villagers who had young children, to announce the opening of the new school. With the warmer weather, and the children not needed at home as much, it seemed a good time to start lessons. In a few months, the youngsters would join their parents in the fields and school would go by the wayside until harvest was over.

Joseph headed to his study to read the morning mail before they left. He shuffled the stack of missives as he entered the room. He rounded the desk and settled into his chair, dropping the pile on his desk.

He leaned back and thought about the investigation thus far. Grundell hadn't yet presented any further information on the person whose background he was investigating. The fall from Samara had been deemed intentional, so now he didn't feel Abigail was safe even with a footman accompanying her.

If the matter wasn't settled soon, he would move his household to London. Or possibly to his Cornwall estate. He would petition the Archbishop to find a replacement for his church. Nothing was worth keeping Abigail in danger. He pinched the bridge of his nose, a headache coming on.

Every day the culprit remained unknown was a chance that whoever wanted to harm her would succeed. Permanently. He pushed his chair back, no longer interested in the morning mail. A decision had to be made directly. If he didn't hear from the investigator soon, he would make arrangements to leave Addysby End. As much as he loved the village and its people, someone here had the capability — and the intent — of ripping his life apart.

A quick glance at his pocket watch urged him to dispense with his plans to do paperwork. It was time to meet Abigail. As he passed the settee, a paper on the floor caught his attention. The maids hadn't been in yet to clean, so he must have dropped it yesterday. He shrugged and picked up the paper, giving it a cursory glance.

His heart did a double beat and he came to an abrupt halt. With shaky fingers he opened it completely. The missive was a letter that had been torn in two, most likely before it would be thrown into the trash. A bold script, parts of sentences missing.

terrible mistake. . . overjoyed to receive your letter . . . My Love Always, Redgrave.

His feet like lead, he stepped backward and dropped into his chair, the paper clenched in his hand. Somehow he'd always expected it would come to this. Abigail could never be satisfied with marriage outside of her class. Rage battled with the fear he'd managed to bury deep inside.

Not only did Redgrave outclass him in position, power, and money, Joseph was unable to even keep his wife safe. He ought to return her to Drake, have him watch over her. The resources of the nobility went well beyond his reach.

Despite his love for his people, he had to face the fact that someone in this village, perhaps even in his own congregation, was trying to kill Abigail. Had she turned to Redgrave because she felt Joseph couldn't safeguard her?

Crushing the paper into a ball, he tossed it in the fireplace and left the room. There would be no peace for him this day.

• • •

Abigail had wanted to travel in the gig for their trip. The openness would allow the warmth of the sun and the essence of the flowers to waft over them. But Joseph was adamant they use the closed carriage. She could only conclude he thought it safer, considering someone was still on the loose with nefarious plans for her.

Abigail breathed in the fresh country air and turned to Joseph. "Can't you just smell the wonderful flowers?"

Joseph grunted.

"I hope the parents are receptive to our visit."

Joseph grunted.

Frustrated, Abigail tried once more. "I wonder if it will be as warm today as it was yesterday."

Joseph grunted again.

Whatever was wrong with the man? He had been fine at breakfast, excited about their visits, anxious to get the children signed up and the school opened. Now, he acted as though she'd done something terrible. Perhaps a direct question would force him to respond with more than a grumble. "Have you word yet on when the new teacher will be arriving?"

"No."

Flummoxed, she leaned back against the squab. Not one to let confusing things lie, she asked, "Is something wrong, Joseph?"

"No."

"Why are you not talking to me?"

"I'm talking."

"That's the first answer you've given me using more than one word."

Silence.

Well, if he wanted to be difficult, fine. She had tried to give him the opportunity to relieve himself of whatever it was that troubled him. She shifted on the seat and looked out the window at the passing scenery. She would not cajole him into pleasantness. She could remain silent herself. Silence was good, refreshing. No need for them to be babbling all the time. Quiet gave one's ears a rest.

Abigail tapped her foot. She crossed and uncrossed her arms. She darted a sideways glance at Joseph. His lips were tight, he stared straight ahead. She sighed deeply, glanced at him again. Nothing. She opened her mouth to question him once more when the carriage wheel hit a rut in the road, and she was thrown from her seat. Reaching out for purchase, she grabbed for Joseph, who had moved forward to grab her. Her hand landed in his crotch, his on her breast.

"Are you all right?" He whipped his hand back so fast she jerked and landed on the floor, her skirts sliding up to the top of her thighs.

Blushing, she drew her skirts down. "I am fine."

"Good." He extended his hand to help her up.

"Are you all right?" She settled on the seat and smoothed her skirts, then adjusted her hat.

"Fine."

She tugged on her jacket. "Splendid. I am thrilled that we are all so fine."

"Abigail . . ."

Raising her chin, she assessed him coolly under lowered lids. "Yes?"

Joseph shook his head, and gazed out the window. "Never mind."

· · ·

He was sick at heart. Although at the beginning of their marriage, he'd thought Abigail still in love with Redgrave, the last several weeks he'd put the man and their erstwhile betrothal from his mind. Things had appeared to be going very well for him and Abigail. While she no longer seemed to consider their marriage as being merely friends working together, neither had she given him a reason to believe she'd changed her mind about not wanting more from their relationship.

He'd been a fool to think Abigail had recovered from the heartbreak of being jilted, or the sudden departure from the *ton* and all things familiar. But for the cad to write to her. And it appeared that she had written to him first. His muscles tightened in anger. Redgrave's profession of love for a married woman, while he was a married man, was abhorrent to Joseph's way of thinking.

But what of Abigail? The note seemed to be in response to a missive she'd sent to him. Were they planning a lovers tryst? But everything he knew of Abigail cried out that she was much too honorable for deception. He pinched the bridge of his nose with his index finger and thumb. A headache was definitely on its way.

The afternoon passed with stilted conversation between the two of them when they were alone, and cheerfulness as they visited the families. He ached to mention the letter, but was deathly fearful of the conversation that would result. Sometimes ignorance was preferable.

If I don't cease this ruminating I will surely be a candidate for Bedlam.

Later that afternoon, completely exhausted, he and Abigail alighted the carriage in front of the house and ambled up the stairs. The strain of the day had indeed, resulted in a rather brutal headache. Abigail held herself stiffly, neither one of them touching.

"I am quite fatigued. I would prefer a dinner tray in our room," she said, her face pinched.

He nodded his consent, wondering if she also preferred solitude.

So she can dream about all that she'd lost?

Chapter Sixteen

Abigail was already in bed when Joseph entered their room later that night. She'd left an oil lamp burning, but had pulled the bed hangings closed, and was resting on her side, her back to Joseph's share of the bed.

She'd spent the hours since they'd arrived home going over their conversation that morning, trying to determine what it was that had changed Joseph's mood. No matter how many times she ran it through her mind, she came up with no answers. He had been fine at breakfast, then cool and remote once he'd joined her for their trip.

Busy with her thoughts, she jerked when the bed coverings slid open and the mattress dipped, announcing Joseph's presence. She held her breath as he settled in. The warmth of his skin soothed her as his leg rested next to hers.

Just about every night of their marriage, he'd reached for her. The only time she could remember him not initiating intimacy were the times she'd been injured. Would he do so tonight?

Her question was answered almost before the thought had completely formed in her mind. Joseph placed his warm hand on her hip and leaned down to kiss her shoulder. "Are you asleep?"

She rolled over onto her back and studied him. "No."

He lowered his head and took her mouth in a soft, seeking kiss. His lovemaking was almost sad—as if he'd lost something, which saddened her as well. Slow and gentle, with definitely a part of him missing.

Barely a few minutes after he collapsed on top of her, he cupped her cheek and left the bed, pulling the curtains closed. Within seconds she heard the rustle of his dressing gown and the click of the door latch.

Frustrated, she considered following him to wherever he'd hied off to and demanding he tell her what in heaven's name was wrong with him. However, she was exhausted from the tension of the day, so she kept to the bed. She would insist on answers in the morning.

She took deep breaths until she felt her muscles relax. Despite her angst, within minutes, she drifted off to sleep.

• • •

Joseph reached for his glass of brandy and wandered to the window. Nothingness greeted him. Complete darkness. No shadows danced on the other side of the glass. Exactly how he felt, dark and shadowed.

For the first time since their marriage, intimacy with his wife had been unsatisfactory. He'd tried to push Redgrave to the back of his mind, but every kiss, every caress, every touch reminded him that Abigail wanted another man. Whether she had actually betrayed him or not didn't even seem as important as the fact that she'd contacted Redgrave.

Would their relationship always be relegated to a part of her mind that only brought her familiarity and companionship? Would he always be second best to a man who had disgraced her?

He tossed back the brandy and slammed the glass down on the window sill, the sound echoing in the dark room. Leaning his forehead against the glass he closed his eyes and tried very hard to block from his mind *My Love Always, Redgrave.*

• • •

Ready to do battle, Abigail entered the breakfast room the next morning. Joseph had apparently come to bed sometime during the night, but was gone when she awoke. No longer would she allow this stalemate to continue. This was not a game of chess, but her life, and not one to permit unsolved situations to linger, she would demand to know exactly what happened between breakfast yesterday, and their trip to the village.

She stepped through the door, mouth opened, prepared to order Joseph to explain immediately what was troubling him. She came to an abrupt halt at the empty room. She swung around and faced Manning. "Has Mr. Fox eaten breakfast already?"

"Yes, my lady. He breakfasted earlier and was called away to speak with one of the villagers. I believe there was a problem with a youth and a young girl."

"Thank you." She felt as though all the air was let out of her lungs.

"I will send hot tea in for you, my lady."

She nodded and took her seat, reaching for a piece of toast. "And some fresh toast, please."

Fidgeting in her seat once she had finished her tea and toast, and with no idea how long Joseph would be away, taking a brisk walk in the gardens seemed the only way to release some of her pent-up agitation at being denied a good argument. She pushed her chair back before the footman could assist her and strode from the room.

An hour later, feeling no more settled, she returned to the house and climbed the stairs to her sitting room. She padded to her writing desk and withdrew a piece of vellum. Picking up a pen, she dipped it into the inkwell and began to scribble. Her thoughts drifted to Joseph. His smile, his tenderness, and caring. How he'd held her when she'd been afraid, carried her when she'd been injured, and had refused to leave her bedside when she'd been ill.

He was dedicating his life to helping people. To making sure those who needed comfort received it. That the children were well cared for and educated. While the men of the *ton* were more interested in their tailor and their clubs, he wanted to make a least a little corner of the world a better place. So much about the man was to be admired and loved. She stopped abruptly, her eyes widening in surprise.

Oh, dear. What I promised myself would never happen, had indeed come to pass. I am in love with Joseph.

Not the heady type of love she'd thought she'd felt for Redgrave. Now that she had lived with Joseph these months, her love for him was a much deeper, satisfying one. The sort of emotion that one knew would last forever.

Then as if a cloud had passed overhead, blocking the sunshine from her window, she felt a chill. At one time she would have thought sharing her feelings with Joseph would have brought him happiness. Although he'd never spoken the words, she knew in her heart Joseph loved her. Undoubtedly, her insistence on their marriage being one of friendship had kept him from speaking the words what were so obvious from his actions.

Until yesterday. All the easy companionship and passion they'd shared had vanished. Last night's lovemaking had been missing something that had always been there before. A connection, a closeness that she'd only felt with Joseph. Tears rimmed her eyes at the loss, and she feared she would never get it back again. How could she correct a problem when she had no idea what it was?

• • •

Joseph dragged himself out of the carriage and up the stairs. Young John Drayton had compromised Elizabeth Warren, and they would be married as soon as the banns were called.

He'd arrived at Ben Warren's home with Drayton sitting upright in a chair, sporting a black eye and bruised chin, eying Warren with trepidation. With the wringing of her hands, and tears coursing down Elizabeth's cheeks, it didn't take much to surmise what the situation was.

At least Drayton had assured Joseph that he had fully intended to ask for Elizabeth's hand before her father had used his fists to encourage him. They were young, but very much in love, so he was sure they would deal well with each other.

Now to handle the problem with his own shattered marriage. Somewhere between the Warren house and his own, he'd decided to confront Abigail with her perfidy. As difficult as the confrontation would be, clearing the air and finding out exactly what her feelings were in regard to the cad was necessary.

"Is her ladyship about, Manning?" he asked as the butler helped him off with his jacket and took his hat and gloves.

"Lady Abigail is in her sitting room, sir."

Joseph nodded his thanks and trudged up the stairs to the first floor. As determined as he was, his feet dragged, each step toward her room feeling as though he was mired in mud. He tapped briefly on the door, then entered at her beck.

Abigail sat at her escritoire, pen in hand. Glancing up, she blushed and immediately thrust the paper into the middle desk drawer.

He felt all the blood drain from his face. "What is that you were writing, my dear?"

She shook her head. "Nothing. Just a letter to Penelope."

Extending his hand, he walked toward her. "May I see it?"

"No." She moved away from the desk, agitation in her every step. "Did you resolve the problem that called you away?"

"Yes. John Drayton and Elizabeth Warren will be joined in holy matrimony as soon as the banns are read."

"I am glad it is all settled."

"A problem easily solved." He paused and rested his hands on his hips. "Unlike our own problems."

Anger flashed in her eyes, and she turned on him. "I have no idea what *problems* you refer to, sir."

He sauntered toward her. "Are you sure about that, Lady Abigail?"

She moved away. "I am quite sure, sir."

"Indeed." He nodded toward her desk. "Perhaps that paper you hastily shoved into the drawer has something to do with our *problem*."

Two bright spots of red appeared on her cheek, and she began to twist her fingers. "My letter to Penelope?"

"Don't do this, Abigail. Please don't pretend ignorance. It doesn't suit you."

She crossed her arms over her middle, as if to protect herself. "I have no idea why you are so upset about my letter. And furthermore, I insist on knowing why you have been so cold and remote since yesterday."

"Let's see. Maybe a *letter* has something to do with it?"

Abigail shook her head. "You are not making sense, Joseph."

"All right. Since you insist on playing this game, I will come right out with it." He ran his fingers through his hair, then stared directly into her eyes. "I know about Redgrave."

Abigail's brows drew together. "Redgrave?"

"Yes, my dear. Redgrave. The man to whom you were betrothed."

"Of course you know about Redgrave. Drake told you all about him before we were married. Whyever would you bring him up now?"

Joseph chuckled without mirth. "I don't know. Perhaps if you gave it some thought, you might come up with the answer to your question."

She stared at him open-mouthed. "I have absolutely no idea what you are talking about."

"I saw it, Abigail!"

"Saw what?"

"The letter."

"What letter?"

"The letter from him."

"From whom?"

"Redgrave!"

They continued to stare at each other across the open space between them. Seconds ticked by, the only sound in the room their heavy breathing.

"You are making no sense whatsoever. There is not, nor was there ever, a letter from Redgrave."

"My respect for you is diminishing by the minute."

"How dare you!" She drew herself up. "If anyone's respect is being questioned, it is mine for you." She leaned forward, her hands fisted at her side. "Once again I will reiterate. I have no idea what you mean."

"Fine. Have it your way. If you want to conduct a separate life, then there isn't much I can do, is there?" He pinched the bridge of his nose. "I have decided to send you back to London."

Her head snapped back. "London? Why?"

"I have failed miserably in keeping you safe. I also think your life is there. It appears you are missing those you've left behind."

Abigail crossed her arms and tapped her foot. "Why do I have the feeling I've wandered onto the stage of a bad play? You are spewing lines at me, and I have no idea what my response is supposed to be."

"All right. In plain English, this will not work. I am very sorry that I somehow don't meet your expectations, but I cannot be something I am not, have never been, and will never be. No matter how much I . . ."

"Joseph . . ." She reached out to him, but he turned his back.

With an anguished cry, she whipped past him, through the door, slamming it on her way out. He cringed with the noise, his heart sickened by their exchange. His world was crumbling around him. Everything he thought he had, and that he had thanked God every day for, had turned to dust. Their marriage was a sham, and she could very well die tomorrow from another bullet or fire.

As a married woman, once she was back in London she would no longer be under the cloak of scandal. Deep down, he'd always questioned the success of this marriage. She was too far above him in station and no doubt missed all the better things in life that Redgrave would have provided for her.

He wandered down to the library, and poured a brandy. Glancing out the window, he noted a soft rain had begun to fall. He had no idea where Abigail had gone off to, but hopefully she had not gone outdoors. Then he shook himself. Why did he care? He'd caught her right in the middle of writing to her potential lover.

He leaned back in his chair, his eyes closed. Memories of Abigail from the time she was a little girl, following him and Drake around until they were forced to tie her to a tree to keep her from annoying them, had him smiling. Then as a young lady, preparing for her come-out, telling him she wanted to dance her first waltz with him. Her young, loving heart had shone in her eyes that night. It had torn him apart to rebuff her, telling her he was much too old to be dancing with debutantes.

He'd been forced to watch the young men line up to request dances. She'd smiled and had written names on her card while his gut had tightened. Abigail had not been for him. She was a duke's daughter, and he the son of a rector.

As if someone poked him with a sharp stick, he sat up, placing his glass on the table next to him. What the devil was he thinking? Abigail was not for him? She was his wife! Since when did Joseph Fox give up so easily? And by God, no one, certainly not an upper crust dandy with no respect for women, was going to take her away from him.

He wouldn't be sending her to London. If anything, he would pack up the household and move to Cornwall if that's what it took to keep her safe. And furthermore, he would let her know immediately that it was the end of their "friendship" marriage. He loved her. Plain and simple.

She was worth fighting for and if she felt love was a gamble, then let the battle commence. If it took the rest of their life together, he would once again see that love in her eyes that he had refused all those years ago.

Suddenly anxious to see her, and let her know where he stood, he headed back to her sitting room. She hadn't returned yet. Wanting a frontal attack, he made his way to the desk, pulled out the drawer and removed the paper she'd hidden from him. Taking a deep breath, he held it in shaky hands and began to read.

Oh, God.

His mouth dried up and his eyes misted as he read Abigail's scrawl. She'd drawn various sized hearts over the paper with "Abigail loves Joseph" written inside each one, like a young miss in the schoolroom. With the way he'd been behaving all afternoon, it was no wonder she'd attempted to hide it from him.

A sense of euphoria washed over him, causing him to grin and want to shout out loud. There apparently would be no battle, since it seemed he'd already outflanked the enemy, and the war had been won.

Chapter Seventeen

Abigail flew past Manning at the door. He quickly opened it, his eyebrows raised. "My lady, it is beginning to rain."

She shook her head and continued on, not daring to speak lest she burst into tears. She had no idea where she was headed, only that she had to get away from Joseph. For some unfathomable reason, he believed her to be in touch with that bounder, Redgrave. As if she were stupid enough to want to deal with that man ever again.

Perhaps she had never stated it, but surely Joseph must have noticed her feelings for him had changed. How could she love him so much and have him not trust her? He hadn't bothered to explain why Redgrave had even come up. She hadn't thought of the man in weeks.

Right now all she wanted to do was hide. Hide from his accusations and the hurt she'd seen in his eyes. Perhaps she should have behaved like an adult and stayed at home, insisting Joseph tell her why in heaven's name he thought she had anything to do with Redgrave. After she managed to calm down, she would return, and demand he tell her what he was talking about. If she had to tie him to a chair in order to get him to do it, then that was what she would do.

Not sure where she intended to go, she headed toward the village. She needed to walk off her anger. A soft rain had begun to fall, and combined with the layer of clouds above, the dark and dreary afternoon fit her mood. She ran her palms up and down her arms, but the chill came from deep inside her.

Thoughts racing through her mind, she was surprised to note she'd reached the edge of the village. She slowed her walk, then hesitated when a carriage drew up alongside her. Assuming it was Joseph, she picked up her pace again, her face forward, not wanting to acknowledge him. Let him begin the conversation.

"Lady Abigail!"

Abigail turned to see Lady Durham waving to her from the window of her carriage. "Come in out of the rain."

Groaning inwardly, Abigail stopped and regarded the woman. She would indeed appear foolish if she continued walking with the rain growing steadier every minute, but she was in no mood for conversation. And where in heaven's name would she tell the woman she was off to in this weather? Drat running into her just now.

Resigned to her fate, she accepted the driver's hand and climbed into the coach. "I'm sorry to get your carriage all wet. I didn't realize it was about to rain when I left the house." She smoothed the wet ringlets from her forehead and attempted a smile.

Lady Durham just stared at her, a slight smile teasing

her lips. The carriage started with a jerk.

"Thank you for offering a ride." Abigail wiped the water from her face, feeling particularly silly at being caught in these circumstances.

No response from her hostess.

Growing a bit awkward, Abigail said, "I was planning a trip to the circulating library, if your driver will be so good as to drop me off there."

Nothing.

A tad alarmed, she clasped her hands in her lap. "Is everything all right, Lady Durham?"

"Actually, Lady Abigail, everything is wonderful. Finding you here in the rain on the road, by yourself, is probably the best thing that has happened to me since your arrival in Addysby End."

Abigail tilted her head in question. "I'm afraid I don't understand."

"No worries, my dear. I will be more than happy to explain."

Abigail shifted in her seat, edging her way toward the door. Whatever was the matter with Lady Durham, she didn't want any part of it. Although she would never call the woman a close friend, she'd never had a reason to wonder about her.

Until now.

"Actually, since I'm already so wet, and I'm sure to damage your lovely seats, if you will instruct your driver to stop, I would prefer to walk."

"I don't think so."

Abigail lunged for the door handle just as Lady Durham reached under her seat and withdrew a pistol, aiming it directly at Abigail. "Sit back, please."

Her mouth dried up as she stared at the gun facing her. Her fear increased when she noted how steadily Lady Durham held the weapon. The woman was no stranger to firearms. "What is this all about? What do you want from me?"

"Dead, my dear. I want you dead. My feeble attempts to get rid of you thus far have been unsuccessful. This time there will be no rescue, or poorly aimed bullets."

Abigail gasped, suddenly realizing the person behind all her mishaps was sitting directly across from her. "It was you. All along, it was you causing my accidents."

Lady Durham broke into a smile. "Very good, Lady Abigail." She dipped her head as though receiving a great honor.

"Why?"

"A minute, if you please. There is something I need to take care of first." She thumped on the ceiling of the carriage, and it came to a rolling stop. "This pistol will be pointed directly at you, so I suggest you sit back and wait. Quietly."

Once the driver arrived at the door of the carriage, Lady Durham placed the hand holding the pistol alongside her, with the barrel of the gun pointed directly at Abigail. "Martin, I have changed my mind. Instead of heading home, I prefer a ride along the river. I will instruct you when to stop."

"It's raining a bit hard now, my lady."

"I don't pay you to argue with me, or to point out things that I have no problem seeing for myself," she snapped. "Just get back up on your perch and drive."

The driver tugged on his forelock. "Yes, my lady."

Abigail's head was spinning. All along it had been this woman behind her accidents. What could she have possibly gained?

"While we take our little journey, I will appease your curiosity." Once again she drew the pistol up so it sat snug in her lap, aimed at Abigail's chest.

"You see, *Lady Abigail*, unlike you, I was not born into wealth and privilege. I had to fight my way up from the mud to become Lady Durham. I won't bother you with the details, since I'm sure your tender sensibilities would be shocked. And we cannot have that, can we?"

Keep her talking. Abigail needed to figure a way out of this mess. As long as Lady Durham continued to prattle on, she had time. And surely she wouldn't be foolish enough to shoot her right here in the carriage where blood would splatter all over. She gulped. Better not to allow her thoughts to wander in that direction.

"My husband, Lord Durham, was a shriveled-up, old, decrepit man. I'm not even sure he knew he had married me. I had been companion to his wife, and once she died, I stepped right into her role."

Abigail glanced out the window, noticing the river, the water gushing and swollen from recent rains. Small sticks and branches floated by, tumbling and rolling, as if on a race to the end. The carriage remained on the road that ran parallel to the waterway.

"Once the old bastard died, he left me with nothing. Nothing! Do you know how many times I had to wipe his slobbering mouth because he refused to hire a nurse? I should have known then that he'd wasted away whatever money he'd had."

Abigail tried to control her breathing so she could think. The panic racing through her was jumbling her thoughts. For as many times as Lady Durham had attempted to kill her, there was no doubt in her mind that unless Abigail gained control, she would very shortly be dead.

And she would never see Joseph again. Before she had time to tell him how much she loved him, and how happy—not merely content—she was with her life. They would never hold each other in the night and whisper plans of the future. Tears rushed to her eyes when she thought about how much she was destined to miss if this deranged woman had her way.

Lady Durham continued her discourse. "Then he cocked up his toes and within days his heir, a snooty nephew from Lancashire, showed up and invited me to leave the premises." She shook her head, her lips pinched. "All he gave me, besides a boot in the arse, was a portion, paid monthly." Lady Durham's eyes flashed. "That is not what I'd worked so hard for. A tiny monthly sum? Not at all."

"What has that got to do with me?"

"You don't know? My goodness, *Lady Abigail*, you are not as smart as I thought."

Nothing the woman said made sense. How trying to kill her would improve Lady Durham's circumstances was a puzzle. Then she remembered her visit to the circulating library when she'd first arrived and Mr. Fogel's words when he had met her.

We were all happy to hear Mr. Fox had married. Although I'm sure some of the ladies who had their eye on him weren't too pleased.

Abigail's eyes met Lady Durham's. "Oh."

"Exactly." The woman's smile was reminiscent of pictures she'd seen of the devil, teeth flashing, eyes snapping.

I am in a lot of trouble.

• • •

Spurred into motion, Joseph strode from Abigail's sitting room and rushed down the stairs. "Manning, has her ladyship left the house?"

"Yes, sir, she has. I warned her that it had begun to rain, but she continued on, anyway."

"When?"

"About a half hour past, sir."

If he took his horse, Whitney, he would get soaked, but the carriage couldn't go places the horse could and would also slow him down. Since he had no idea which direction Abigail had gone in, Whitney was a better idea.

Shrugging into his coat, he stepped to the door, then stopped and addressed Manning. "If her ladyship returns, please see that she stays put."

His agitated stride ate up the distance between the house and the stables. "Tack up Whitney for me," he snapped as he entered the area.

The stable master, Jackson, viewed him with surprise. "Are you sure you want to take Whitney out in this, sir? The carriage might be a better idea."

"No. Tack him up, please. I want to leave immediately."

"Yes, sir."

"Jackson, did her ladyship take Samara this afternoon?" If Abigail was on foot, she couldn't have gotten too far in the short time since she'd run from the house.

"Haven't seen Lady Abigail today, sir."

Joseph nodded and accepted the reins from the stable master. He vaulted onto Whitney's back, patting the horse's neck as the animal shifted back and forth, picking up on his master's agitation. Guessing she would have headed to the village where she could get some type of shelter, he squeezed his knees against the animal and took off in that direction.

The light rain had turned into a full drizzle by the time he arrived at the village. He drew up the collar of his jacket to keep the rain from sliding down his back. Muddy water splashed up from Whitney's hooves as he slowed the horse to a walk. He stopped and eyed the store-lined street. No shoppers were about, either having sought refuge in one of the stores, or returned to their warm and dry homes.

He would have to go from one store to the next in his search. But whatever it took, he would do it. He had no idea what that letter was about, but it was obvious Abigail was stunned at his accusations, and if he hadn't been such an ass, he would have realized she knew nothing about the note. Now he would be lucky if she didn't pack up and leave him.

Although there was absolutely no proof, he couldn't help but consider the letter was left there on purpose, and was somehow connected to her accidents. So few people had access to his study that he found it difficult to imagine who'd left it there.

A frantic hour later, soaked to the skin and twisted with fear, he left the last business. A thorough search had resulted in nothing. No one in the village had seen her, and she hadn't visited any of the stores. A numbing dread swept over him at the possibility that she had met with yet another accident. What a fool he'd been to let her run off like that.

He pulled the brim of his hat low and turned Whitney in the direction of home. Hopefully, Abigail had walked off her anger and returned to the house. It was the thought of her back, safe and sound, lounging in a hot bath that kept him from losing all control.

• • •

Lady Durham thumped on the ceiling of the carriage, never letting her gaze shift from Abigail. "I had it all planned out. Once my mourning period had ended, I would marry Joseph and have all that lovely money. But instead, he travels to London to find sponsors for his bloody school and comes home with a wife!"

The carriage came to a rolling halt. "I suggest you climb down like the lady you are, and not utter a word to my driver. Not that he would help you. He's much too stupid to understand anything."

The door opened, and Lady Durham once again tucked the pistol out of the driver's sight. Abigail accepted the man's hand and stepped down, quickly appraising the area. They were on a rather lonely road, with woods on either side. Straight ahead, through the woods, the river raged.

Lady Durham linked her arm into Abigail's. "Let's take a stroll, shall we?"

If the driver saw anything odd about his mistress and her guest walking through the woods toward the river in the pouring rain, he never presented an inkling of curiosity. He faced forward, with the water dripping from the brim of his hat, not acknowledging them at all.

Chilled to the bone, Abigail shook from the combination

of cold and fear. She could bolt and run, but she had a suspicion Lady Durham knew how to use that gun. Of course, if she immediately dodged behind trees, she might avoid being killed, but with her gown dragging in the mud, sopping wet, she probably wouldn't be able to move very fast, anyway.

"Well, my dear, here we are."

They'd stopped at the edge of the river. Abigail's stomach dropped as she viewed the angry, swollen water racing past them. She didn't want to die. Even though Joseph had accused her of terrible things, they could settle their differences. She loved him, and despite this recent dispute, she knew he loved her.

"Lady Durham, you don't want to do this."

Edith's eyes rose in apparent genuine surprise. Was she truly so without conscience? "Whyever not?"

"Because Joseph already knows someone is trying to kill me. He won't view another accident as such. He will hire someone. They will find you."

Edith smiled sweetly. "Not when I show up as the grieving friend, crying my heart out for my dear, dear friend, *Lady Abigail*. So sad. So young, and lovely. *Tsk, tsk*."

Before Abigail could say another word, her head exploded with pain, and everything went black.

• • •

Joseph was sick to his soul. It had been three hours since Abigail had left, and he had no idea where she was. After returning from his search of the village, he'd dried off, changed his clothing and paced until he could stand it no longer, then he left again. He'd scoured the countryside with no results.

Of course, had she been angry enough, she could have taken refuge in one of the abandoned cottages strewn throughout the wooded area. He glanced out the window. The rain had not eased up. If she didn't return soon, she'd likely develop a lung fever which would take her life as easy as any of the accidents she'd had.

Twice he'd gone to the side table and poured himself a brandy, and both times he'd left it sitting. As much as the liquor would calm his nerves, he needed to stay alert. Chances were something serious had happened to her. Once more, his muscles clenched and he cursed the foolish words he'd flung at her.

A pounding at the front door had him racing from the library to the entrance hall. Manning had already opened the door when he arrived. Jake McCray, a local farmer, stood on his doorstep, his wet hair plastered to his forehead. Muddy water pooled at his feet as he hovered in the doorway. In his arms, he held a pale, soaking wet, still as death, Abigail.

Chapter Eighteen

"My God, Abigail!" Joseph rushed forward and took her limp body from the farmer's arms. "What happened? Where did you find her?"

McCray stayed on the doorstep. "Sir, I don't want to wet your floor, and I'm pretty muddy besides."

"I don't care," Joseph panted as he shifted Abigail against him. She was cold as marble, her face blanched white. Unsure at this point if she was even alive, he was anxious to get her upstairs and warmed. "Please, come in anyway."

Manning sent one of the footmen for towels.

"Please follow me," Joseph said as he bounded up the stairs. One of the maids jumped when he gained the first floor, then hurried in front of him to open the bedchamber door. "Thank you. Please have the footmen start a fire in here immediately. Then send Sanders to me after you arrange for hot water to be brought up for her ladyship."

Out of breath after the race up the stairs and rapid

instructions to the maid, he struggled to gulp in air as he laid Abigail gently on the bed.

"Are you sure you want me in her ladyship's bedroom, sir?" McCray asked from outside the door, his hat crushed in his beefy hands.

"Absolutely. I need to hear what happened." The very last thing he was concerned about right now was any mess the man might leave behind.

Joseph placed his hand on Abigail's chest and closed his eyes with relief at her steady breathing.

"Oh my, sir. What has happened this time?" Sanders bustled into the room, her hands clutching her throat.

"I'm about to find out, Sanders. Right now I want you to remove all of these wet clothes and dry your lady off. I'm afraid I've wet the bed linens, as well. Just get her cleaned up and dry." He smoothed back the hair from her forehead. "We need to send for the doctor, once again."

"I already sent for the doctor when Manning told me about my lady's condition."

"Thank you." Joseph turned to the farmer still hovering in the doorway. "I'm sorry to be so muddle-headed, but perhaps it is best if we retire to the library while her ladyship's maid attends her."

Once they descended the stairs, Joseph instructed Manning to bring some dry clothes for McCray to the library.

He poured them both a glass of brandy and handed it to the man, noticing how his own hand shook. "This will help." Joseph swirled the liquid, then spoke. "Tell me what happened."

"I was out in my field, right by the river there, when I looked up to see something floating in the water. I thought my eyes deceived me that it was a woman, face up, being bumped along."

Joseph cringed at the vision. "Go on."

"I ran alongside her for a bit, then grabbed onto a low hanging branch and made my way out to the water. It was moving quickly, so I had to hurry. I grabbed her hand, and pulled her toward me. Once I had her out of the water, I noticed the back of her head was bleeding."

Joseph's head jerked up from where he had been studying the pattern in the carpet as he listened to the man's tale.

"Bleeding?"

"Yes, sir. It looked to me like she got a good whack on the back of her head. Either before she fell in the water or from a rock in the river." McCray took a sip of his brandy. "After I pulled her out of the water, I recognized her right away as your wife. So I fetched my wagon and brought her here."

"I am eternally grateful to you, McCray. If there is anything I can do for you, please just ask."

"Sir, the doctor is on his way, and a hot bath has been set up in the blue guest room for Mr. McCray to clean up and change into dry clothes," Manning said as he entered the room.

"Thank you, Manning."

"There's no need to do that, sir. I'll just be on my way. I'm glad the missus is home where she belongs." McCray placed his glass on the table and said, "I can't imagine why she was floating in the river, but it looks like some bad things to me, sir."

"I can't thank you enough." Joseph shook the man's

hand, and accompanied him to the door. Once he'd taken his leave, Joseph climbed the stairs, once again chastising himself for taking such poor care of his wife.

Their bedchamber was warm and dimly lit. Abigail lay on the bed, the covers pulled up to her neck. Her stillness shattered him, and in that instant he decided to leave Addysby End. As soon as Abigail was recovered, he would send a missive to the Archbishop and request a replacement. Then they would move the household to Cornwall. Far away from all the misery and pain that had plagued her since her arrival.

"Has there been any word from the doctor?"

"Not yet, sir," Sanders whispered.

Joseph sat alongside Abigail, memories of previous vigils all too fresh. *Never again.* They would move from here, and she would be safe even if he had to return her to her family. "I'm so sorry, my love. I've failed you again. Not only failed you, but drove you from your own home and right into danger once more with my ridiculous accusations." He brought her cold hand to his cheek.

Whatever it took he would gain Abigail's forgiveness. Even if she had written to Redgrave, which was becoming more uncertain since he had time to think about it, that no longer mattered. Redgrave was no longer a threat. Joseph would build their love…after he got on his knees to beg her forgiveness.

"The doctor has arrived," Manning said walking up quietly to the bedside.

Giving her one last glance, Joseph left the room, determination in his every step.

Later, he sat in front of the fire in the library, studying the dancing flames. Orange, red and blue tongues of heat engulfed the coals like guilt consumed his person. His clasped hands dangled between his spread legs. Why did love have to hurt so much?

Not love, lackwit, but well-deserved guilt at your mistrust.

Nothing had happened between him and Abigail to warrant his suspicions. Despite the note, it was beyond the pale to assume Abigail, who had never given him leave to distrust her, would betray her vows. He would get to the bottom of it as soon as he was assured she would recover from this latest trouble. Despite not understanding why, all of his instincts cried out that her accidents were somehow tied to the note.

He checked his pocket watch, amazed that barely forty minutes had passed since he'd left the doctor with Abigail. Each minute was an agony of self-torture.

The doctor entered the room at a brisk pace. "Mr. Fox, I've determined there is no major damage to your wife's lungs. Apparently the man who rescued her from the river had enough knowledge to press on her back to release whatever water she might have inhaled."

Joseph nodded his wish for the doctor to continue.

"However, she is not yet awake, most likely due to a blow to the head when she fell."

"Or was pushed."

The doctor frowned, obviously taken aback. "Have you any reason to believe Lady Abigail was the victim of an assault?"

"Every reason in the world, only I cannot prove it. Either my wife is the clumsiest, most inept woman in all of England, or someone wishes her harm."

The doctor thought for a moment. "Have you reported your concerns to the constabulary?"

"Yes. As well as engaging the services of a man from London to investigate." Joseph paused to run his fingers through his hair. "How soon can she be moved?"

"It is hard to say. I will tell you she should not be moved until she has awakened. Were you planning a trip?"

"My household will be moving to Cornwall as soon as she has recovered sufficiently."

The doctor shook his head slightly. "We will certainly hate to see you leave, Mr. Fox. Addysby End will be a lesser place with your absence. However, in light of what you have just told me, I understand your desire to move your wife to safety." The doctor gripped his medical bag and headed toward the door. "I will check on her tomorrow."

"Thank you. Can I offer you a bit of brandy before you leave?"

"No. It has been a rather long day for me, and I feel the need to seek my bed. I'm afraid brandy will have me falling asleep on my horse."

"I'm happy to send you home in our carriage."

"Thank you, but I will be fine." The doctor nodded. "Good night."

• • •

Abigail's eyelashes fluttered, the pain at even that small

movement shooting from the back of her head to her jaw. Easing her lids closed again, she tried very hard to focus on where she was, and why she hurt so. Her atempt to determine what had happened produced an agony so sharp she welcomed the return of the darkness that shrouded her. She would solve the riddle of her pain later.

Unaware of how much time had passed since she'd last awakened, Abigail tried once more to open her eyes. The pain was still there, but not quite as sharp as before, more of a throbbing ache. Moonlight confirmed it was the middle of the night. Slowly, she eased her head to the side. Joseph sat slumped in a chair next to the bed. A smile teased her lips at his disheveled state.

His was in disarray, apparently from having run his fingers through his hair numerous times. It had been a while since he'd shaved, his cravat was missing, and his shirt winkled beyond relief. The familiar sound of his soft snores comforted her.

A wave of sadness washed over her as she watched him. A thought tickled the edge of her mind, an important issue between them. Did that have something to do with her head aching? If only she could persuade her hand to reach out and touch him, gain his attention. There was an important matter she needed to discuss with him, but she couldn't recall what it was. Tears of frustration gathered in her eyes.

Not wanting to tax her brain further, she once more welcomed the darkness.

• • •

Joseph awoke with a start. His heart sped up as his eyes

riveted on Abigail. She lay as still as death, apparently not having awakened. He laid his hand gently on her chest, the slight movement assuring him she hadn't died in the night. Grasping her cool, limp hand in his, he kissed her knuckles, hoping somewhere inside her she felt his love.

Love that he had yet to admit. But no more. She would know of his love, and if she continued to insist that she didn't want love in their marriage, despite her scribbles to the contrary, he would do whatever it took to change her mind. After all, they had the rest of their lives.

Perhaps a trip to the continent before they settled in Cornwall. Time to just be together, make love all day, attend the theater, enjoy some of the finer foods of France. Now that Napoleon had been defeated, they could travel freely.

Manning approached Abigail's bedside, his usual respectful demeanor more troubled.

"Sir, Lady Durham has arrived, asking after her ladyship."

"I don't want to see anyone now." He shook his head and waved at the butler.

"I indicated as such, but the lady is most insistent she can help."

"Help? What the devil is she talking about?"

"She is apparently under the impression that my lady is still missing."

He rubbed his tired eyes with his thumbs. Perhaps Lady Durham had some information about Abigail's near drowning that would help solve the riddle. "Very well, I will speak with her."

Joseph descended the stairs as Lady Durham eyed the entrance hall, almost as if she were viewing it for the first time. Her eyes glowed and she tapped her foot in impatience. In all, she appeared as if she could barely contain a great secret.

"Lady Durham."

Her expression immediately changed to one of sorrow and pain. The shift was miraculous, and were he not so distraught and eager to have her leave, he would have dwelled on the rapid adjustment.

"Mr. Fox, I am so very upset to discover that Lady Abigail is missing. As soon as I heard the unwelcome news, I hurried right here to see what I could do to help. I'm sure you are beside yourself with worry, and no doubt need someone to comfort you at this time."

Her words all rushed together, almost as if they had been practiced many times. The hairs on the back of his neck rose, but he shook off the feeling. He was, indeed, beside himself.

"I am pleased to inform you that her ladyship is home."

Her breath hitched and her face paled. She licked her lips and appeared to have difficulty accessing air for her lungs. "Indeed? I hope all is well?"

"Actually, she was returned to me unconscious. Farmer McCray arrived with her last evening. He pulled her from the river."

Lady Durham's palm covered her mouth. "Heavens! Is she. . .?"

Joseph shook his head. "She is still unconscious. The doctor has been here, and says we must wait."

Color returning to her face, she inhaled deeply and blew out a breath. "I insist on staying and tending to her. You have obviously not had enough sleep or food. You must take care of yourself, and I will sit by Lady Abigail's bedside."

Joseph hesitated at Lady Durham's suggestion. The uncomfortable feeling lingered, but he dismissed it with a shake of his head. "That would be most welcomed, my lady."

"Good. Then it is settled. I will sit by your wife's side while you enjoy a nice hot bath and breakfast. I will guard her very carefully, I assure you."

Side-by-side they ascended the stairs, Joseph's uneasiness increasing with each step. Lady Durham chatted merrily as they reached the corridor and continued on down to the bedchamber.

Abigail lay motionless on the bed, not having moved from the position he'd left her in. Joseph reached her side and smoothed back the hair from her forehead. Leaning down, he kissed her on the cheek. "Please come back to me, my love."

He glanced up in time to see Lady Durham's lips tighten and her eyes narrow. She quickly smiled at him. "She will be fine. Now you go enjoy your breakfast."

Joseph nodded as the door opened and Sanders entered, balancing a bowl of water and several cloths.

"Good morning, sir. How is our lady today?"

"The same, I'm afraid."

Sanders curtsied briefly to Lady Durham and moved around the bed to place her supplies on the small table next to Abigail's head.

"I would be happy to administer to Lady Abigail," Lady Durham said. "I am sure you have other duties to attend to."

"There are no other duties more important than my lady." Sanders dipped the cloth into the water and wrung it out.

Feeling a bit more secure with Sanders nearby, and

still not sure why, he left the room, closing the door quietly behind him.

. . .

After a quick wash and shave, Joseph sat at the breakfast table, pushing his food around his plate, his appetite non-existent. Shoving his dish away, he drew his coffee cup closer as Manning entered the room.

"Sir, Mr. Grundell requests an audience."

At last. Maybe some news.

"Excellent. Send the man in."

Perhaps Grundell had finally gotten to the bottom of Abigail's accidents. Joseph rose as the investigator entered and shook his hand.

After the usual greetings, and with a coffee cup in front of each man, Joseph leaned forward, his elbows on the table. "I am hoping you have some news for me. Abigail has been involved in yet another accident, and I am beside myself trying to figure this out."

"I am so sorry to hear that. Actually I do have news. I am not completely sure this person is responsible for your wife's accidents, but she has a very interesting background."

"She?"

"Yes." He opened his notebook, adjusted his spectacles and flipped the pages. "Lady Edith Durham started out her life as Bessie Mayer, daughter of the town drunk."

"Lady Durham?" His eyes flicked upward to the ceiling where he'd left Abigail in her care. The uneasiness he'd felt before returned.

"Yes. The lady has been living a very different life than

the one she was born into. Apparently, after a very suspicious fire, in which her father, Eddy Mayer, died, she disappeared."

Joseph took a sip of his coffee, the uneasiness turning into a cold sense of dread in his stomach.

"She turned up in London, as a clerk in a woman's store. I spoke at some length with an employee there. Through Lady Edith Durham's work at this ladies' store, she obtained a job as companion to Lady Durham." He raised his eyes, and added, "That would be her deceased husband's first wife."

Joseph indicated the man should continue.

"Although there was nothing strange about that woman's death, since she was under doctor's care for a bad heart, Lady Edith Durham married the late Lord Durham only a few weeks after her employer's death."

Joseph stood, unable to sit as he listened to the litany of events that was leading up to God knew what.

"What has all of this to do with my wife's accidents?"

Grundell leaned back and crossed his arms. "Lady Durham was almost forcibly removed from the Durham Estate by the new heir—the old man's nephew. As far as I can tell, she receives a very small monthly portion from him."

"I am not sure this means anything," Joseph said, trying desperately to make sense of the information.

"I don't know for sure myself, sir. However, given the mystery surrounding your wife's accidents after she suddenly appeared in Addysby End as your wife, I thought you should know."

Joseph expelled a breath of air and collapsed into his chair. Thank goodness Sanders was with Abigail. Even though all of this did not exactly make Lady Durham the guilty party, it certainly gave him something to discuss with the constabulary.

"Sir, Lady Durham has requested a tray be sent to her in my lady's bedchamber," Sanders said as she entered the breakfast room.

Joseph shot out of his seat. "Is she alone with Lady Abigail?"

"Yes. . ." She barely got the word out when he raced past her, almost knocking her off her feet.

Chapter Nineteen

Abigail opened her eyes. Her head still hurt like the devil, but she didn't feel quite so muddle headed. Her gaze roamed the room and settled on Lady Durham standing at the door. The woman was speaking to someone, and then Abigail heard the sound of the bedchamber door closing and footsteps hurrying away down the corridor.

As Lady Durham turned back to her, Abigail sucked in a deep breath, memories of being led to the bank of the river, and then her head exploding in pain, swamping her. She opened her mouth to scream as Lady Durham whipped the pillow out from under her head and placed it over her face, pressing hard. "This time I will be sure that you're dead, you little bitch."

Abigail tried to move her head to the side but her neck wouldn't cooperate. She brought her hands up and pushed, allowing her to get a lungful of air before the pillow came down on her face once more.

She raised her knee and shoved it into Lady Durham's stomach. The woman grunted, and her hold on the pillow lessened, but with persistence she pressed down again.

Abigail twisted and turned, fighting for her life. The harder she fought, the more determined were the hands that pressed the pillow on her face. Soon the lack of air and her weakened state got the better of her. She no longer had the strength to resist.

So here she would die. In her own bed before she could tell Joseph how much she loved him, and how sorry she was for whatever it was that had caused their rift. She should have remained and insisted on knowing exactly of what she was being accused, instead of fleeing like a child.

Abigail attempted once more to make her arms move to push the pillow away, but black dots gathered at the edges of her eyes and slowly moved to engulf her.

• • •

Joseph flung open the door to their bedchamber. An agonized cry erupted from his throat at the sight of Lady Durham holding a pillow over Abigail's head.

Within seconds he was across the room and grabbing the woman by her shoulders. He wrenched her to the side, and she stumbled to her knees. "Get out!" he shouted in Lady Durham's direction.

"No!" She snarled and jumped up. She threw herself on Abigail who was struggling to sit up, gasping for breath. "She has to die."

Still breathing heavily, but with strength that amazed him, Abigail kicked out, catching Lady Durham in the chest.

The woman flew backward and landed on her bottom.

Joseph scooped Abigail into his arms. "Manning!" He bellowed.

Flush faced and panting, Grundell and Manning burst into the room, Grundell with a pistol in his hand. Lady Durham screeched and scrambled up, attempting to run from the room. The two men grabbed her and pulled her hands behind her back.

Joseph collapsed on the bed, settling Abigail on his lap. His stomach knotted and he watched in fear as she opened her eyes, the color slowly returning to her face. "Oh, my love," he groaned.

"Joseph . . ."

He shook his head. "No. Don't speak, please don't speak. Just breathe, and let me look at you."

She moved her hand to cover his where he held her tightly. Her chest rose and fell as she tried to get her breathing under control. Two tears tracked down her cheeks. She'd never looked more beautiful, and he had never loved her more than he did at this moment. And it was beyond time to tell her, to take the step that would lay his heart open. No matter what had happened in the past, or the differences in their station, he knew in his heart they were meant to be together.

With a groan, Abigail shifted and sat up, resting her head on his shoulder. He rocked her back and forth, as if she were a babe. Grundell and Manning left the room, dragging a cursing Lady Durham between them.

Slowly Abigail's breathing returned to normal, and she looked up at him. "I love you, Joseph." She swallowed, her voice raspy as she continued, "I was so frightened that I would never have the chance to tell you. I am still not sure what our disagreement was about, but know this. I have never loved anyone as I love you."

"I know." He closed his eyes. "We will sort it all out, but my love for you is strong enough to weather any storm."

Manning returned to the room, followed by Sanders. "My lady, it is with great happiness that I find you awake and looking as lovely as ever."

Abigail laughed, her voice still scratchy. "Manning, I am sure I look anything but lovely, but nevertheless, I will accept your compliment."

"Mr. Grundell asked me to inform you that he has taken Lady Durham to the magistrate."

"Thank you." Joseph rested his cheek on Abigail's head, thankful it was all over. Suddenly aware that Abigail was draped all over him, in her nightclothes, with both Manning and Sanders beaming at her with delight, Joseph rallied himself and addressed Sanders. "Please prepare a bath for her ladyship."

$$\cdots$$

Refreshed from her bath, and after a light breakfast of tea and toast in her room, Abigail headed to the library where Manning told her Joseph was meeting with the magistrate, Mr. Kerns.

Still a bit weakened from her ordeal, but the pounding in her head now reduced to a steady low pain, she opened the door to see him in deep conversation with Mr. Kerns. Joseph left the magistrate and hurried to her. "How are you feeling, my love?"

"I still have a bit of a headache, but I do want to speak

with Mr. Kerns."

The gentleman bowed. "And I wish to speak with you as well, Lady Abigail. I am very sorry for your trouble. But be assured we will get to the bottom of this."

Joseph assisted her to the settee where she sat, easing back carefully.

Mr. Kerns proceeded to question her, and between Abigail and Joseph the entire story unfolded, beginning with the shooting in the woods to the attempted smothering in her own bed.

"Nasty business," Mr. Kerns said as he shook his head and closed his notebook.

"What will happen to Lady Durham?" Abigail asked.

"Once I received the note from Mr. Fox, I arranged to have Lady Durham held in her home until we got to the bottom of this. Her family has been notified, and we'll see from there what our recourse will be."

"I was under the impression she had no family." Hands joined, Joseph and Abigail walked with the magistrate slowly to the door.

"Her late husband's nephew, the new Lord Durham, has been sent word. It is up to him what he wants to do with her. Most likely a private sanitarium if he wants to part with the funds." He shrugged. "Most times women of her rank are cosseted away by family members if they're involved in some sort of crime."

All three arrived at the front door. "I will be in touch with you and your wife once this is all squared away." He turned to Abigail. "I am very sorry for all the problems you have had."

"Thank you. I am glad it is finally at an end."

He nodded at them both and took his leave.

Joseph wrapped his arm around Abigail's waist and led her back to the library. Still not feeling quite herself, she rested her head on his shoulder.

"Would you prefer to return to bed?"

"No. I think I would like to stroll in the garden. I feel the need for fresh air."

After obtaining a shawl from Manning, they left the house and wended their way along the rose garden path toward the back of the house. The burned out gardener's shed caused her to shiver. Joseph pulled her close. "I have decided we are leaving Addysby End."

She leaned back to stare at him, eyebrows raised. "When?"

"As soon as I can have the household packed and ready to go." He turned and took both of her hands in his and led them to a stone bench under a large oak tree. "After all that has happened to you, I cannot stay here."

"How long do you intend for us to be gone?"

"Forever." He enveloped her in his arms, hugging her close. "We will move to my estate in Cornwall, or if that doesn't appeal, we can buy something else. Perhaps closer to your family. But away from here."

She shifted to look up at him. "No, Joseph. We can't do that."

"Why not? I will never feel as though you are safe here."

"Lady Durham wished me dead. The woman apparently had designs on you and your money. When I showed up to interfere with her plans, she took it upon herself to get rid of me. She has been stopped. The authorities will deal with her now. There is no reason to give up your dream of providing a school for the village children."

"You are more important to me than any dream I might have had."

She smiled and brushed back the hair forever falling on his forehead. "Let us not discuss this now. Once we have had the opportunity to put this behind us, we can make a decision. But first I want you to explain to me what it was that caused you to accuse me of dallying with Redgrave."

He sighed and looked out into the distance. "I found part of a note on the floor in my study. It had been torn and appeared to have been dropped. From what I could read it seemed as though you and Redgrave had been corresponding. In the note he referred to his 'eternal love' for you—or some such thing."

Abigail's jaw dropped. "That is ridiculous. I haven't heard from that bounder since he absconded with Lady Priscilla." Heat rose from her middle, and she jerked her chin upward. "If he had the audacity to actually contact me, I would send him a blistering retort that would burn his fingers to hold it."

"I believe you, and I am so sorry I didn't dismiss the note out of hand." He kissed her knuckles. "Will you ever forgive me?"

"Since I am quite sure the note was planted by Lady Durham, I can understand your acrimony." She took both of his hands in her, squeezing lightly. "But surely you know I would never betray you, Joseph."

"I know, my love. The fault rests with me. I fear it was always in the back of my mind that our difference in rank would one day cause you to regret your hasty decision to marry me. That somehow you would feel as though you had settled." He held up his hand as she started to speak. "My feelings for you go back years. When you were about to make your come-out, I wanted nothing more than to sweep you away and have you for my own. But I knew as the daughter of a duke, your life was destined to be far away from mine."

"Oh, Joseph. You know my family. It would not have made a difference."

"A young man's insecurity, I'm afraid."

"Then I guess we owe Redgrave a great deal of thanks. When you acted as though you had nothing more than brotherly feelings for me, I decided to find a man who I could care for as much as I cared for you." She smiled softly. "Not only was that man not Redgrave, but his deception brought us together as we should have been long ago."

"I shall send him a case of the finest brandy in the morning."

Abigail grinned and dipped her chin. "With my compliments."

They sat in silence for a few more minutes, then Abigail said, "Now I think I should enjoy a brief rest. I find I am still weary from my dunk in the river." She raised the back of her hand over her mouth to quell a yawn.

Joseph moved so quickly he almost knocked her to the ground. "And I shall join you. As I feel quite fatigued myself."

She raised her eyebrows, a siren's smile playing on her lips. "Perhaps we can find a way to pass the time as we wait for sleep."

He drew her up. "An excellent suggestion, and one that was on the tip of my tongue, my lady."

"Then lead the way, sir."

Abigail chuckled when his steps hurried as he directed her toward the house.

Epilogue

Two months later

"You will be happy to know that Lady Durham is ensconced on an estate near the Scotland border." Joseph entered Abigail's sitting room with a letter in his hand. He'd been expecting word from the magistrate any day, and he was only too happy to receive it and relate the information to his wife.

"Is she now?"

"Yes." He glanced at the missive. "It seems Lord Durham had a cottage out that way before he became the current lord. He writes that the estate is not large, but Lady Durham will have no use of a carriage, so she will not be able to leave the area unless she walks."

"You know, in some ways I feel sorry for her."

"Surely you do not mean that. The woman tried to kill you. More than once."

"I know. I am not saying she doesn't deserve what she got, and in some ways it should be more, but anyone who will go to those measures must have been desperate, indeed."

Joseph pulled up a chair to sit in front of her writing desk. "I know as a rector, I should be forgiving, but I cannot bring myself to excuse what she did."

"She told me she had a very difficult early life. It seems she struggled quite a bit to get as far as she did."

"I know. Mr. Grundell had a full report on her. But being poor and coming from dire circumstances doesn't push one past the line of considering murder. That is a step that very few people can take."

"I am just glad it is all over. Things have been so peaceful."

He left his seat and moved around the desk. Resting his hip on the desk, he swung his leg back and forth, regarding her. "I must say that peace agrees with you. There is a glow about you that I have never seen before."

"Ah. The glow. Yes, that is probably apparent, at this point."

He pulled her up, settling her between his spread legs, wrapping his arms around her waist. "And what mysterious business would create such a glow?"

She began to fiddle with his cravat, a smile teasing her lips. "Something very serious, yet it will make you happy."

"Serious? Is that right?" He ran his palms up her arms to rest his intertwined fingers at the back of her neck. He pulled her forward and rested his forehead against hers. "You already make me happy."

He leaned in and kissed her sweet lips. Never again would he want to live through the horror of Abigail's accidents.

He'd felt so useless and inept. She was his entire world, and he didn't care who knew it. He looked in the mirror each morning and admitted out loud that he was besotted. "So what is this serious matter that makes you glow?"

Once again she fiddled with is cravat. "Suppose I tell you that in about seven months there will be a new person living in our house."

His heart leapt. A baby! He had guessed that's where she was leading him, but didn't want to get his hopes up.

"A new person? Is your mother coming for a visit?"

"Joseph!"

"What?"

"You know what I mean."

He sighed. "Yes, I guess I do. I'm so sorry, Abigail I will miss you dreadfully." He kissed her on her nose and walked toward the door.

"Joseph! What are you talking about?"

Turning toward her, he said, "Why our agreement, of course."

"What agreement?" She followed behind him as he left the room and walked to his bedchamber.

He got as far as his door and turned to her. "Why our agreement that I will no longer trouble you with *my attentions* once you are *enceinte*."

"What?" Her brows furrowed, and then she made a circle with her lips. "Oh."

"Yes, my love. I will shake your hand and wish you a good night." He took her limp hand in his, shook it, and entered the room, closing the door in her face.

Within seconds he opened it up, pulled her through and wrapped her in his arms. "I decided I am not as honorable as I thought. I won't stick with our agreement." He took her face in his hands and kissed her gently. "I want you right beside me in my bed every night for the rest of our lives." She sighed and leaned on his chest. "If you insist, my love."

"I do. Indeed."

Extra content

February, 1816
Addysby End, England

Abigail awoke from a frantic dream where she'd gone to the village to shop and arrived back home without her baby. She had not even missed the infant until they'd sat down to dinner and Joseph asked her where the babe was. The panic at his question had set her heart to pounding, which caused her to awaken.

She jolted up in bed, her breathing rapid. "Oh good heavens, Joseph, I've had another one of those nightmares."

His warm hand rested on her shoulder. "I'm sorry, sweetheart. No doubt all your numerous worries about the babe hinders a restful sleep."

Abigail shifted in the bed to face him, her huge belly keeping her husband a goodly distance from her. "If this child doesn't arrive soon, I'm afraid my body will explode." She waved to her middle. "Have you ever seen such a sight in your life?"

His eyes warm with love, he rested his hand on her bulge and smiled. "No. But I love the sight of my wife carrying my child."

Abigail eased up and swung her legs over the edge of the bed. "Well, perhaps we can arrange for *you* to carry your child for a while. Goodness, I am enormous."

"Not enormous, my love, glowing with good health and motherly love."

"Ha."

"Mr. Fox, Mr. Fox!"

• • •

Joseph jumped from the bed and slid into his banyan on his way to the door. "Yes?"

"I am so sorry to disturb you and her ladyship, but the constabulary, Mr. Bullfinch, is downstairs and wants to speak with you immediately." Manning's usual placid demeanor had been shattered by something akin to a disaster, given his state.

"Please ask the man to step into my study, and I will be with him shortly."

"Do hurry, sir. The damage . . ."

Joseph shut the door on the man's words, then paused and frowned. *Damage? What the devil is going on downstairs?*

"Joseph? What was that all about?" Abigail grunted as she pitched her body forward, grabbing onto the bedpost to keep herself erect.

"I'm not sure. But Manning is all in a dither, and wants me to present myself to the constabulary post haste."

After a quick wash and dress, Joseph hurried down the stairs to the sound of something crashing to the floor in the kitchen. Grunts and flesh hitting flesh followed.

"I'll teach ya to go around breakin' decent people's belongins!" More stumbling and crashing into things had him wincing.

"Cease immediately, or I shall lock the two of you up and throw away the key." Bullfinch's voice carried over the melee as Joseph strode into the kitchen.

"What is going on here?" All action ceased as Joseph took in the picture. Cook stood wringing her hands while Mr. Bullfinch glowered at two boys, perhaps eight or nine years of age, both with blue eyes, blond hair, and freckles. They glared at each other, their fists at the ready.

Their wiry frames were in severe need of some nourishment and their clothing was filthy, torn, and worn out. Both faces were smeared with dirt.

"Who are you and what are you doing creating this havoc in my home?"

They dropped their fists, and moving together, slung their arms around each other shoulders. "We're here because this bloke," the boy who spoke jerked his head in Bullfinch's direction, "said you could straighten us out."

Joseph placed his hands on his hips and swung his gaze in the constabulary's direction. When the man just stood there glaring at the boys, Joseph said, "Speak, man."

"Can we step into your study, Mr. Fox?"

"And leave these two ruffians alone with my cook? I think not." Joseph crossed his arms and leaned against the counter. When one of the boys reached for an apple in a bowl on the table, he snapped, "Don't."

The boy drew his hand back.

"You two will march to the sink over there," Joseph nodded in the direction of the sink next to the cook, "and wash your hands. Then you will politely sit at the work table and my cook will fix you something to eat."

When the boys grumbled, he added, "Now. Or there will be no food."

They shuffled to the sink, one of them shoving the other away as they made a feeble attempt to clean themselves up.

"Now, Mr. Bullfinch, I suggest you relate to me exactly what this is all about."

"These boys were found sneaking into the kitchen at the Inn. Mrs. Mosner was chasing them with a broom when I arrived for a bit of breakfast."

"And why did you bring them here?"

Bullfinch ran his fingers through his hair. "They said their mother died a few months ago, and they've been on their own searching for their father since then."

"And?"

"Well, I couldn't just leave them to wander about. They've no money, and no idea where this 'father' is. I thought, since you've started that school, that you might take control of them."

"Control of them?"

"You know, Mr. Fox, maybe set them to work in the house, or the school. Keep them fed and such until we can decide what to do with them."

Joseph pulled out a chair, and turning it around, sat with his arms braced against the top of the back. He peered at the boys. "What are you names?"

One boy opened his mouth to speak until his brother shoved his elbow into his side. "Don't say nothing to the bloke. Just eat up and we'll be on our way."

"And where is it you're headed?"

Silence reigned as they shoveled the bread and cheese into their mouths, heads down. They ate as if they hadn't a meal in days.

"Well Bullfinch, it appears they are not interested in any help I can provide. I suggest you ship them off to the Canterbury Goal, where they will be shackled in irons and left to rot." Joseph made to leave the room. He winked at Bullfinch as one of the boys yelled, "Wait."

"Who are these boys?" Abigail entered the kitchen, her belly leading the way. "I heard the racket all the way upstairs."

"Aren't you a fat one," one boy said.

Abigail rested her hands on her stomach and stared him in the eye. "And aren't you a rude one."

The second boy slapped his brother on the head, and within seconds they were scrapping, rolling on the floor.

Joseph reached down and grabbed each boy by the scruff of his neck and hauled them up. "Apologize to my wife. Now."

"I didn't do nothing. It was him."

"Bullfinch, take them away."

The constabulary grabbed each boy by the arm and headed to the door.

"My apologies, mum." The boy rubbed his tattered sleeve on his nose while he spoke, making it difficult to know if that's what he had actually said.

Abigail regarded the child. "I accept your apology." She placed her hands on the boys' heads and led them back to the table. "Do you think you can finish your meal without fighting if Mr. Fox and I leave you here for a minute?"

They both nodded, once again grabbing for the food. Cook had added sausages, potatoes, and eggs to their plates, and they consumed it all with enthusiasm.

"Mr. Fox?" Abigail motioned toward the door. She, Joseph, and Bullfinch crowded into the small study. "*What* is going on, Joseph?

Joseph tilted his head in Bullfinch's direction. "Would you care to enlighten both of us?"

"I'm so sorry to disturb you, Lady Abigail." He took a quick glance at her belly, his face reddening. "I had no idea you were … that is …"

"I am with child, Mr. Bullfinch. I can assure you it is not a contagious condition."

If possible, his face reddened further until Joseph was afraid the man would suffer an apoplexy.

"No, my lady. Of course not." Inhaling deeply, he continued. "These boys were found attempting to steal from the Inn's kitchen. The story they tell me is their mother died a few months ago, and they are looking for their father."

"Oh my goodness. They are little boys! They've been on their own for months? That's terrible."

"But you still haven't explained fully why you brought them to me," Joseph said.

"I cannot send them to the gaol, and if they make their

way to London, they will end up in a workshop laboring eighteen hours a day."

"Is London where they say their father is?"

"I doubt there is a father. At least none that they are aware of. According to the little the lads have told me, there has been no father in the home their entire lives."

Abigail reached for her handkerchief and dabbed her eyes. "Oh, my. That is so sad. The poor little mites."

A thunderous crash, strong enough to shake the floor stopped all conversation.

Abigail clumsily rose to her feet. "What in heaven's name was that?"

"Most likely the *poor little mites*." Joseph wrenched open the door and headed to the kitchen.

. . .

Two weeks later they had settled into a routine. David and Daniel, the twins of eight years who had come so uproariously into their lives, were trying their best, but months on their own had given them quite a few bad habits. And Abigail had every reason to believe these habits that been with them well before their mother died.

"David, I told you to carry a handkerchief with you at all times. It's not proper for a young man to be wiping his nose on this sleeve." She pulled a clean handkerchief she'd tucked into her sleeve for this very purpose and handed it to the boy.

"My apologies, mum."

"It is 'my apologies, my lady'," Joseph said, entering the breakfast room.

"Yes, sir." Both boys cast their eyes to their plates.

A lack of a man in their lives had left the boys with a fear of Joseph even while they competed with each other for his attention.

"Have you finished your chores?"

"Yes sir." In unison.

"Good. As soon as I am through with breakfast we will begin your riding lessons."

Two pairs of blue eyes opened wide. "For sure, sir?" Daniel said.

"Yes. You have both been trying very hard. Lady Abigail and I are pleased with your progress. But remember, it is off to school for your lessons once we are through riding."

Two pairs of young shoulders slumped.

Abigail did her best to hide her grin. The girls who attended their school took to their lessons quickly, enjoying the instructions and the camaraderie with the other girls. Most of the boys, however, including the twins, preferred outside activities to sitting at a table doing their sums, or struggling to read the Bible.

David and Daniel had indeed been trying very hard. They had kept their fisticuffs down to just a few a day, and their little bodies had even begun to fill out. They no longer had such the scrawny look about them.

"What are your plans for today, my love?"

Pulled from her musing, she regarded her husband. "There is not a great deal I can do right now." She shifted in her seat, but no position seemed comfortable anymore.

"When I return for luncheon I will escort you on a stroll in the garden."

"That will be nice."

"We're finished, sir." David eyed him with the impatience of youth.

"I am not finished. While you wait for me, you may go to the stables and have Jackson begin your lesson on preparing your horse for a ride."

They both jumped up and raced for the door, shoving each other aside.

"Come back here." Abigail used what the boys called her "bossy" voice.

They shuffled back, heads hung low.

"Do you wish to have your very first riding lesson canceled before it starts?"

"No, mum. I mean, no, my lady."

"Good. Now leave the room like two gentlemen."

They walked to the door. Daniel held his head high and bowed at David, who bowed back and they left the room.

Abigail and Joseph grinned at each other.

"I received a note from the vicar of St. George's Church in Sowerset Green."

"Where the boys lived?"

"Yes. The mother took in washing and sewing to support them. She died of consumption three months ago, and the boys just up and disappeared. Mr. Grant was happy to hear they are here with us."

"No other family?"

"No. Mr. Grant had never seen a man about the place, and the mother didn't attend church, so he never got to know her very well."

"What now?"

"I don't know. I'm still muddling it over."

Abigail placed her hand over his. "You know what we

must do, don't you?"

After a moment, he nodded. "There seems to be no other way."

. . .

The following week, Abigail lay on her back in bed, observing her enormous belly. In this position, not only could she not see her feet, the protuberance blocked the rest of the room from her view. She sighed, and moved to get up when a sharp pain shot across her stomach.

She grabbed her belly and held her breath until it passed. This was too soon! The babe wasn't due for another month. She took deep breaths to calm herself.

Joseph had already left the room, headed to breakfast. She didn't want to alarm him, and perhaps the twinge was not one of many. She shifted to her side and waited. About five minutes later, another pain started in her back and shot to the front. Gripping her stomach, she squeezed her eyes shut, trying to block out the pain. It didn't work.

A fine sheen of perspiration covered her body. Gently, she eased up off the bed and held onto the bedpost. Taking a deep breath, she stood. Everything seemed to be all right. She made her way over to the bell pull to ring for Sanders. No sooner had she rung, then another pain gripped her. Apparently her labor had begun. Ready or not, the babe was on its way.

"Oh, my lady, what is wrong, you are very pale." Sanders dropped the towels she'd been holding and rushed to her side.

"I am not sure, but it appears the babe will be making its

entrance into the world today."

Sanders covered her mouth with her fingers. "Goodness. I must notify Mr. Fox. And he must send for the midwife."

"Yes, yes. That is a good idea." She barely got the words out as another pain washed over her, a whimper escaping from her mouth.

"Here, my lady, let me help you back to the bed before I see to Mr. Fox."

Abigail nodded and lumbered across the room. She gingerly lowered her body to the bed, then placed her palms on her belly. "Perhaps you had better hurry, Sanders."

The maid raced from the room, leaving her mistress sweating and panting.

"Please God, make all be well with the babe."

"Abigail!" Joseph skidded into the room, Daniel and David on his heels. "Are you all right?"

"Yes. I am fine, but I think your child has decided he has had enough and wants to meet us."

"But it is too soon!"

"I know that, but I believe he doesn't really care." Her last words were lost as she fought another pain. "I think you should send for the midwife."

"I have. Manning dispatched a footman."

Daniel and David stared wide-eyed at Abigail, clutching each other's hands.

"Boys, I think it best if you both ran along to the school. Tell Mrs. Marks that I will not be there today." Joseph spoke over his shoulder as he patted Abigail's hand.

"Is the baby coming, sir?"

"It appears that way. And this is no place for you now. Please do as I asked."

"This is no place for you, either," Abigail said.

"I will not leave until the midwife arrives."

Sanders hurried into the room, laden with cloths. "Mr. Fox, I need to prepare her ladyship. You must leave us now."

"No. I'll not leave until the midwife is here with her."

Abigail sat straight up and moaned as another pain hit. "Please, Joseph, Sanders is here. I would feel much more comfortable if you were not a witness to this."

He reached up and tucked an errant curl behind her ear, smiling devilishly. "I was there at the beginning, my love."

"Oh. You are wicked."

His grin confirmed her observation.

"My lady, the midwife has arrived. She will be up shortly. Right now she is giving instructions to Cook." Manning made a quick retreat once his message had been delivered.

"Joseph, please?" Her face twisted as another pain washed over her.

"All right, sweetheart. I'll leave you now. But I will be downstairs in my study."

• • •

Joseph turned from his place at the window as Drake and Penelope entered the drawing room. Manchester carried Robert, with Penelope and her huge belly following. The nanny brought up the rear. Abigail's brother and sister-in-law had arrived just in time for a visit.

"How is she?" Penelope asked as she settled on the settee with her husband's assistance.

"It has been hours. I am about to burst into that room and see what the devil is taking so long."

Penelope grinned. "It does take a while, Joseph. Luckily Drake was passed out for most of Robert's birth."

"Yes, I have heard the tale. Injury from a fall, and a bit too much brandy to ease the pain."

"Sir, has the baby arrived yet?" Daniel raced into the room, knocking over a small table in his wake. David followed behind, no less frantic.

"Not yet, boys."

"Who have we here?" Drake asked.

"This is Daniel and David Locke. They have been staying with us since their mother passed away." Joseph turned to the boys. "This is the Duke and Duchess of Manchester. You must bow to both of them."

Wide-eyed, the boys bowed, then stared at the couple.

"It is not polite to stare."

"Oh. Sorry, sir." David lowered his eyes, but continued to cast glances at his guests.

Joseph's head jerked at the sound. "Is that a baby crying?"

The room grew silent.

"Yes. I believe it is." Drake grinned at Joseph.

"Sir, you may see your wife. The birth is finished." Sanders' smile stretched from ear to ear.

Joseph strode from the room with Drake, Penelope, David, and Daniel behind him like chicks following a mother hen.

They marched up the stairs, then Joseph quietly opened the door.

Abigail sat up in the bed, propped up on pillows. Her tired face was aglow. She held in her arms two little bundles.

Two?

Joseph's heart did a rapid double time. "Two?" Was that his voice squeaking like that?

"Yes, my love. Two." Abigail grinned. "Come meet your two sons."

"Twin boys?"

She nodded, tears forming in her eyes.

Drake and Penelope moved to the bed. Joseph eased the blanket aside on each babe. "They are beautiful."

Drake slapped him on the back. "Well done, Joseph. Congratulations."

They all admired the babies, with Joseph and Abigail counting fingers and toes. They were all there.

Joseph leaned back and his gaze caught David and Daniel standing near the door, looking as if they were ready to bolt.

"What is the matter with the both of you? Come here and see the babies."

They both shook their heads.

Sharing a glance with Abigail, Joseph left her side and walked to the boys. He squatted down and looked them in the eye. "What is wrong?"

"Nothing," David said.

"Daniel?" Joseph asked.

"We were just wondering, sir."

"Wondering what?"

The two young boys looked at each other. Clearing his throat, Daniel asked. "When will you be sending us away, sir?"

"Away?"

"Yes." David said. "We figured now that you had two of your own twins you don't want us hanging around here."

Abigail shifted one of the babies, and held out her hand. "Come here, boys."

They shuffled their way over.

"Sit here." She patted the bed alongside her.

"Oh no, my lady. We couldn't sit on your bed."

"Yes, you can. I have invited you to do so."

They sat stiffly next to her, Daniel wiping his nose with his sleeve. Abigail raised her brows, and the boy hung his head.

"Look at me."

They both looked up as she took Joseph's hand. "You two are not going anywhere. Mr. Fox and I talked it over and decided we want you to say here with us. To be part of our family."

"Really?" Daniel asked.

"Yes. Really. And now that Lady Abigail and I have another pair of twins, you can teach them all about being boys."

"I think we can do that, don't you David?" Daniel said.

"Sure. And we have some new tricks we just learned…"

David stopped speaking as Joseph glared at him.

"Well, maybe we won't show the babies our new tricks."

"Good idea."

Aknowledgements

Of course I think my book is wonderful when I finish it, but alas, that is seldom true. So many other people are involved in the process. I would like to acknowledge them here.

First off, my beta reader, and husband of thirty- seven years, Doug. He doesn't know that I came up with the idea of him being a beta reader as a way to get him to read my books. Since his literary choices tend to run toward the classics, it was no mean feat. Whatever works. Thanks for your input.

My fabulous critique partner, Char Chaffin, slaps my hand and cuts me off from overused words on a regular basis. Without her insight and expertise this writing journey would be very different.

Two fabulous ladies who take my offering and turn it into something better are my editor, Erin McCormack-Molta and editorial director, Gwen Hayes. Thanks for having those polishing cloths at the ready.

My brother, Brian, spent twenty-five years battling fires as an inner city firefighter. His willingness to share his expertise was invaluable. Thanks for the quick phone calls with the 'can this happen?' questions.

I have a group of ladies whose support means more to me than I can say. They cheer me when I'm on top, and talk me off the ledge when I'm down. Thanks, Unicorns. Love you all.

A special acknowledgement to Kay Rogal and Patti Shenberger, two lovely women who left this earth much too early. You will always be Unicorns, ladies. Enjoy the rainbow.

The Beau Monde group is comprised of so many regency experts that it boggles the mind. Ask a simple question and several immediately respond with extensive information from their wealth of knowledge. Thanks for all the responses to "just one more question."

And to my street team, Callie's Cohorts, thanks for all your hard work in helping to promote my books.

About the Author

Callie Hutton always knew those stories she made up in her head would be written down one day. There was nowhere else for them to go. After years of writing articles and interviews for magazines and company newsletters, she wrote her first novel. With twelve books under her belt, and a few more contracted, the relief at having somewhere to tell those stories is wonderful. She lives in Oklahoma with her husband, daughter, and two dogs. Her son and his wife are awaiting the birth of twin boys.

She is past president of the Oklahoma chapter of The Romance Writers of America, and *USA Today* bestselling author of *The Elusive Wife*, the first book in the Marriage Mart Mayhem series.

You can catch her hanging out at Facebook, Twitter, and her home base, www.calliehutton.com. She shares a monthly newsletter with two other authors, and would love for you to sign up to hear about contests, drawings, and new releases.

Sign up for our Steals & Deals newsletter and be the first to hear about 99¢ releases from Callie Hutton and other fantastic Entangled authors!

Reviews help other readers find books. We appreciate all reviews, whether positive or negative. Thank you for reading!

Are you feeling Scandalous?

Our readers know that historical doesn't mean antiquated, that's why they choose Scandalous, an Entangled Publishing imprint, for love stories from eras gone by.

Our romances are bold and sexy and passionate. After all, torrid love affairs are even more illicit when forbidden by social mores. Take a little time for yourself, escape to another era, and discover a timeless romance. There's never been a better time to fall in love.

Never miss a release by subscribing to our newsletter, and join us on our social media pages to keep up with our specials, giveaways, prizes, and what is new with scandalous authors.

Visit our website!

Join us on Facebook!

Follow us on Twitter!

Join our newsletter!

Also by Callie Hutton

THE ELUSIVE WIFE

Newly arrived from the country for the Season, Lady Olivia is appalled to discover that her own husband, Jason Cavendish, Lord Coventry, doesn't even recognize her. She's not about to tell the arrogant arse she's his wife. Instead, she flirts with him by night and has her modiste send her mounting bills to him by day. Hell hath no fury like a woman scorned…too bad this woman finds her husband nearly irresistible.

THE DUKE'S QUANDARY

LONDON, 1814

Drake, Duke of Manchester, has everything planned. This season he'll marry a woman who will be the perfect duchess and a docile wife. Then he's introduced to Penelope Clayton, the socially awkward houseguest his family has tasked him to prepare for the ton. Each lesson draws them closer, and he finds himself unable to resist her. But society can be cruel, and social expectations have a way of making decisions for you.

Also from Scandalous...

LORD OF REGRETS
by Sabrina Darby

Natasha Polinoff's out-of-wedlock pregnancy—which would destroy Lord Marcus Templeton's inheritance—sends her running into the unforgiving night. Now, five years later, Lord Templeton has finally found his beloved. And this time, the viscount will have her. Lord Templeton's arrival fills Natasha with terrible fear... and undeniable longing. He has come to claim her, but she is no mere possession. Lord Templeton will do whatever it takes to bring her back into his arms and back into his bed. Even if it means resorting to blackmail to make Natasha his wife...

MISADVENTURES IN SEDUCTION
by Robyn DeHart

With five siblings to care for, Prudence Hixsby 's duty comes first. But when the eldest — and most cherished — of her younger brothers joins the war, she trades her body for his safety by slipping into the bed of a man whose touch is both fierce and passionate... little knowing she's just seduced the wrong man. Harrison Carlisle, the Duke of Sutcliffe, never imagined that that lovely Prudence would honour his bed and he can't resist her, but he keeps a gentleman's silence. But when Prudence's brother is killed, they find themselves uniting to track down a traitorous murderer.

THE IRRESISTIBLE MISS PEPPIWELL
by Stacy Reid

Dissatisfied with his empty life, Lord Anthony Thornton seeks a deep and lasting connection... and finds himself intrigued by the Ice Maiden of the haute monde. Undaunted by Phillipa Peppiwell's aloof nature and her distaste for the idea of matrimony, he sets out to thaw the bewitching beauty by enticing her with adventures of the most sensual type. But both Anthony and Phillipa hide secrets revealing past scandals best kept buried... and if discovered, could rip them apart.

THE WAGER
by Lily Maxton

Anne Middleton never plays by the rules. She is willful when she should be obedient and unabashed when she should be decorous. Worse still, she can never resist a good wager. Michael Grey—the Earl of Thornhill—knows Anne is no lady of decorum, but her bold impulsiveness slips through his armor, and propriety is forgotten. Roused by heady desire, Michael tempts Anne in a way she cannot resist—a wager. Thus begins a game of chance, where coins have been replaced by a currency that is far more illicit. And the stakes of seduction are dangerous indeed...

If you love Regency Romance, look for these Scandalous titles...

ONCE UPON A WALLFLOWER
by Wendy Lyn Watson

When Mira Fitzhenry's guardian arranges her engagement to one of the most scandalous, yet devastatingly handsome lords to ever grace the peerage, all of society is abuzz. After all, the man has left a trio of dead young women in his wake, including his first fiancée. As the wedding approaches, Nicholas and Mira grow ever closer, yet so does the very real danger. Will the truth bring Nicholas and Mira together or tear their love apart?

TEMPTING BELLA
by Diana Quincy

Mirabella feels nothing but contempt for the man who wed her for her fortune and promptly forgot she existed. Sebastian has been apart from his child bride since their wedding day. When he encounters an enchanting impish beauty at the opera, he's is thrilled to find she is none other than his long-ago bride and he is more than ready to make her his wife in truth.

Too bad the beguiling beauty has no intention of coming meekly to the marriage bed.

Made in the USA
Las Vegas, NV
08 February 2022

43386020R10159